MW01136444

# Could This Be Love

## Praise Him Anyhow Series

# Could This Be Love

## Vanessa Miller

Book 8
Praise Him Anyhow Series

Vanessa Miller
www.vanessamiller.com

Printed in the United States of America
© 2013 by Vanessa Miller

Praise Unlimited Enterprises
Charlotte, NC

Other Books by Vanessa Miller

After the Rain
How Sweet The Sound
Heirs of Rebellion
Feels Like Heaven
Heaven on Earth
The Best of All
Better for Us
Her Good Thing
Long Time Coming
A Promise of Forever Love
A Love for Tomorrow
Yesterday's Promise
Forgotten
Forgiven
Forsaken
Rain for Christmas (Novella)
Through the Storm
Rain Storm
Latter Rain
Abundant Rain
Former Rain


Anthologies (Editor)
Keeping the Faith
Have A Little Faith

This Far by Faith

EBOOKS
Love Isn't Enough
A Mighty Love
The Blessed One (Blessed and Highly Favored series)
The Wild One (Blessed and Highly Favored Series)
The Preacher's Choice (Blessed and Highly Favored Series)
The Politician's Wife (Blessed and Highly Favored Series)
The Playboy's Redemption (Blessed and Highly Favored Series)
Tears Fall at Night (Praise Him Anyhow Series)
Joy Comes in the Morning (Praise Him Anyhow Series)
A Forever Kind of Love (Praise Him Anyhow Series)
Ramsey's Praise (Praise Him Anyhow Series)
Escape to Love (Praise Him Anyhow Series)
Praise For Christmas (Praise Him Anyhow Series)
His Love Walk (Praise Him Anyhow Series)
Could This Be Love (Praise Him Anyhow Series)
Song of Praise (Praise Him Anyhow Series)

To my great aunt, Ruby Knox. She spent ninety long years on earth, but left us for her new home. I will miss her, but consider myself blessed to have had her in my life for as long as I did

# Prologue

"How could this have happened?" Well she knew how it happened, she just wasn't so clear on how she, Raven Thomas, could have been so addle brained as to let it happen.

The pounding on her door caused her to drop the object she had been holding. She rushed to the door and looked through the peephole. It was the Senator. Backing away from the door, Raven hollered out, "You shouldn't be here."

"I won't be ignored, Raven. I'm not leaving until you talk to me."

Fear crept into her heart. She'd seen firsthand what the senator was capable of so there was no way that she was going to go head to head with him on her own.

"I'll break this door down if I have to," he threatened.

Raven picked up her cell phone and dialed Joe Sparrow, one of the associates in her publicity firm. When Joe picked up she quickly told him, "I need you to be a witness to a meeting." Then she flung the door open and said into the phone, "Senator Michael Allen is walking through my front door as we speak. Jot down the time and I will update you later as to how this meeting went."

"Do you want me to turn on the video cam I set up in your house?"

"No, just jot down the time of his arrival. I'll notify you of his departure time."

As she hung up the phone, Senator Allen barked, "Who was that?"

"You don't need to know that. But if I should come up missing, the person who was just on the phone will make sure everyone knows that you had something to do with it."

Taking off his gloves the senator glared at Raven. "I find it sad that after working with me for over a year, you could believe me capable of the things the lame-stream media has tried to pin on me."

"You're forgetting that I researched the incident my-self."

"Yes, and that's what I'm here to talk to you about. When I saw you in the restaurant with your brother, I thought you'd at least have the decency to tell me why your organization has left me to fend for myself."

At fifty-seven the senator was almost twice Raven's age, but the man didn't look a day over forty. He bore a strong resemblance to Dennis Haysbert, that guy in the Allstate commercials. His voice was just as booming and authoritative as the Allstate pitchman's, as well. But Raven wasn't moved. She knew what the senator was and what he had done.

Senator Allen's eyes focused on the object Raven had dropped on the floor. He pointed at it. "Is that what I think it is?"

Raven groaned as she realized the mistake she had made... a mistake that could cost her life. She rushed over to the spot and picked the pregnancy test instrument off the floor.

Before she could dispose of it, the senator grabbed it out of her hands and looked at it. He then turned it so she could see it, as if she hadn't already gawked at it a hundred times. "It's positive."

She didn't respond.

"Is this why you suddenly decided to drop me as a client?"

Raven snatched the pregnancy test out of his hand and then marched over to the door. She swung it open and said, "Leave my house now."

Senator Allen opened his mouth to say something, closed it, then with a look that said he knew exactly what the deal was he said, "This isn't over, not by a long shot."

Raven closed the door behind the senator and then leaned against it with her heart beating so fast she wondered if she needed to call a paramedic. Looking at the pregnancy test in her hand, she shook her head in disbelief. "So it begins."

# Chapter 1

"So what's up, Boss?" Joe Sparrow asked as he came into her office. "I pulled our people off of Senator Allen's case and now he's harassing you?"

"No, he just wanted to know why I decided to end our contract."

"And did you tell him?"

"I think I'll leave that to the authorities. They should be gathering enough evidence to get an indictment soon enough. I just don't think our firm needs to be associated with all that madness."

"Good call." Joe sat down and propped his foot on her desk and then asked, "You really think he did it?"

"Don't you? You were the lead investigator. Every time you turned up new information, what did you tell me?"

"I said it didn't look good for the senator, but that doesn't mean that I'm a hundred percent convinced that he did it... I mean, a pregnant ex-lover on your hands is one thing... murder is a whole 'nother-other."

"Who else stood to gain from that woman's death? It had to be the senator.

"Aren't we jumping the gun here? I mean, who says the mistress is dead? Maybe the senator paid her to leave town and go into hiding."

"I wouldn't put it past the senator to pay a woman to go into hiding, but I don't think it's that simple. I'm telling you, Joe, I know Senator Allen and that woman is dead."

Joe put his feet back on the ground and stood in front of Raven's desk. "And just how well do you know him? Because I'm wondering why he felt comfortable with going to your house. Our clients know that is against the rules."

Raven got up, turned towards the window, stood there looking out at the people as they walked the streets. Since she'd started her career in political public relations, Raven had dreamed of being in the place where politics threw down. The movers and shakers of the universe resided in Washington, D.C. and to be a success, she had to reside here, also.

That had been what she'd told herself, but in light of what she'd allowed to happen, Raven wished she'd never left North Carolina and was still doing public relations for the city government. "I know him... let's just leave it at that."

Shrugging his shoulders, Joe said, "You're the boss."

Yes, she was. And the best thing for her to do now was to get the senator and his family off her mind and concentrate on work. "We have a new client."

"Great! We'll be able to keep the lights on."

"You've got jokes." Raven half smiled, half frowned at that. Because the truth was, her firm needed every client they could get. They'd been in business for three years, but it would take at least five for the firm to turn a serious profit. Raven knew she could make a success out of this business, she just needed the time to do it.

"Who's the client?"

"Judge Linda Hartman."

"Isn't she up for re-election next year? Does she want us to help with her campaign or something?"

"Meet me in the conference room. Let's go talk to her." Raven picked up a file from her desk and strutted out of her office like a woman who was in charge, and very capable of handling her business.

\*\*\*

"We've got trouble," Senator Allen said to his son.

Marcus Allen, the third son of the great and powerful Senator Allen asked, "What kind of trouble?"

"She's pregnant."

Marcus stumbled backward. Grabbed hold of his father's desk to steady himself. "How do you know?"

"Never mind how I know. I just do."

"Okay, so now what?"

"What do you mean, 'now what'? You know what. We've got to do something. This family is on its way to the White House and I'm not about to stand idly by and let anyone get in our way. Not even Raven Thomas... do you understand me?"

Marcus prayed that he didn't understand at all. Because if his father was suggesting what he thought was being suggested... "Let me look into this. You might be totally off base, so just calm down before you stroke out or something."

***

"Judge Hartman, how nice to see you again," Raven said as she shook hands with the formidable judge. "Have a seat."

Judge Hartman sat at the head of the table. Raven sat on her right and Joe took the chair on the left.

"I've watched you over the years, and I'd just like to say that you do this nation proud. I hope to one day see you as a Supreme Court judge," Joe told her. No flattery involved, he meant every word.

"Yes, Judge Hartman, we have a great deal of respect for you and your continued stance on Godly issues that are brought before the court. My step-mother has a great deal of respect for you, also. She says she prays for more judges like you."

"I'm humbled at the high praise, but I have been nothing more than a servant of the Lord for the past twenty years. I can think of no better way to serve Him than in my rulings on the bench. I get tons of grief from the media because of my principles. But they are what they are and as long as my constituents continue to vote for me, I'll keep on doing what I believe to be right."

It was an honor indeed to be sitting in the presence of such a God fearing woman. When Raven was at home, her step-mother, Carmella Marshall-Thomas and her father, Ramsey Thomas provided all the Godly influences that she needed. But being in Washington, D.C., she was short on Godly influences and had allowed herself to forget who she was in Christ. She longed to get back some of what she had lost while in pursuit of her career.

"How can we help you, Your Honor?" Raven asked.

"This isn't easy to talk about," Judge Hartman said as she hung her head, displaying the shame she felt. "My oldest daughter, Britney has always been a bit of a problem child. I've tried everything I can think of to help her, but she rejects all my efforts. Now she's missing and I have no idea what has happened to her. My opponents would love to find her and humiliate me with whatever she has gotten herself involved in."

"Don't worry, Judge Hartman, we will find Britney and we will be discreet about it," Joe assured her.

Judge Hartman stood, shook Raven's and Joe's hands. "I thank you both for your help with this matter. My family means everything to me. I've just never been able to convince Britney of that fact."

As they walked toward the door, Raven said, "To get started we'll need every morsel of information you can give us: Who she hung out with, places she frequented, the last person you saw her with."

Judge Hartman stopped walking and turned to Raven. "I don't know much about my daughter's life these days, but I do know who she was with before she simply vanished."

"Great, who was that?"

"Marcus Allen. They were high school sweethearts. I thought Britney was attempting to rekindle the flame, but after their date, I never heard another word from her."

When Judge Hartman said 'Marcus Allen' the blood drained from Raven's face. She quickly recovered her composure before Judge Hartman noticed any sign of the turmoil going on inside of her. "We'll check with the Lieutenant Governor to see what he has to say about the night he and Britney went out on a date."

"Thank you, Raven." Judge Hartman hugged her. "I knew you were the right person to turn to with this matter. I met your mother and father at a fundraiser last year, so I know you were raised with good, Godly values. The same that my Britney was raised with."

As Raven walked back toward her office thinking about the kind of impression her Holy-Ghost-filled step-mother Carmella Marshall-Thomas must have made on the judge, she almost burst out in tears at the judge's last comment. Because even though she and Britney had been raised in Godly homes, it was obvious that they both had strayed away from the values they had grown up with.

"Speak of the devil," Joe said as he held his hand over the phone receiver. "The Lieutenant Governor is on the phone for you."

Raven knew that Joe was talking about Marcus, and in no way shape or form did she want to speak with him at this point in time. Shaking her head vigorously she rushed into her office. But as it had been lately, God had not made a way of escape for her, because Marcus rang in on her cell. She ignored it and then flipped open her computer to jot down a few things that were on her mind.

Her computer's home page was CNN.com and before she could switch to another site, Raven's eyes gravitated to a big bold headline which read, 'Happening Now. Multi-Millionaire Ronald Thomas is being airlifted from the scene of a horrific car accident'.

Raven wanted to scream. Her life was truly spinning out of control. She already had enough to deal with and now her brother was being airlifted. She clicked on the link as she grabbed her cell phone and dialed her parents.

Her dad picked up. "Hey, Raven, how are you doing?"

"Not too good, Dad. Are you somewhere with a television?"

"Yeah, there's one in this room."

"Turn it to CNN. I think Ronny is being airlifted to the hospital."

Ramsey started stuttering, something about Carmella having a premonition.

"What's wrong?" Raven heard Carmella ask.

"Turn on the television. Put it on CNN," Ramsey told his wife.

Once the television was on, Ramsey told Raven, "We've got it on. Why do you think the person they're airlifting is Ronny?"

"The news reporter ran the plates on the car. The car is in bad shape but it looks like Ronny's Jag."

"Oh my God." Carmella's hand went to her mouth. "My boy has got to be okay, Lord. He's got to be."

"Ronny was just here last week. We had lunch. I can't believe this is happening," Raven said.

With a shaking voice, Ramsey asked, "Can you come home, hon? I think you should be with the family right now."

As her father was asking her to come home, Joe was holding up a piece of paper that told her Marcus was still holding and refusing to hang up until he spoke with her. "I'll be there, Dad. I need to get away from here anyway."

16

# Chapter 2

Raven went online and booked herself on the first flight out of Washington, D.C., headed to Raleigh, NC. She then went home and threw a few items into her suitcase and rushed to the airport. She was glad that she hadn't procrastinated and taken the time to get things in order before jumping on that plane because when she arrived at the hospital, Raven was greeted with the news that Ronny had internal bleeding and had been rushed into surgery.

He was in recovery now and they were all just sitting around his room waiting for his bed to be wheeled in there. "I just can't believe this is happening. Ronny is so full of life. He's got to pull through this."

"He will," Renee, her younger sister said as she put an arm around Raven's shoulder.

"Yes, of course he will," Ramsey assured his children. "Carmella and I have just spent several hours in the chapel praying for Ronny and Jarod. And we know for a fact that

God answers prayers, so everything will be all right." Carmella squeezed his hand as he finished his statement.

Raven whispered to Renee, "Who's Jarod?"

"Nia's son. She's the woman Ronny brought to town to start a business with Mama-Carmella. I think Ronny has eyes for her," Renee said.

Ram, their oldest brother walked over to them and said, "No thinking about it. Ronny is over the moon for the woman."

Before anyone else had a chance to comment on Ronny's love life, the door to his room opened and the guest of honor was wheeled into the room. Ram and his wife, Maxine, Joy and her husband Lance, Dontae and his wife, Jewel, Renee and her husband Jay, Raven and RaShawn stood around the bed looking down at their brother, while Ramsey and Carmella stood back, wiping the tears from their eyes.

Ronny cleared his throat as he told his family, "You all look so beautiful to me. I know I have neglected to spend time with each of you throughout the years, but when I was stuck in that car and thought I was dying, you all were in my heart and my thoughts. I love each of you."

"We love you, too, Ronny. We don't care how busy you are. We know where your heart is," his father told him.

Ronny slowly turned toward his father. "How is Jarod?"

"He's doing fine and waiting for you to get better so you can go on a pirate adventure," a woman who'd just entered the room answered.

Raven figured that she was getting her first glimpse of Nia, the woman Renee and Ram thought had stolen her brother's heart. Not bad, big brother, not bad at all, Raven thought as she noted the love shining brightly through the woman's eyes.

Ronny's head swung around. She moved closer to his bed. "I prayed for Jarod right before I blacked out."

"Thank you," she said, trying to stifle her tears but having a hard time doing so as the tears drifted down her face.

"You were right," he confessed. "I thought I did it all. I didn't think I needed God, but I see now that I would have nothing without Him. God kept me alive and I will never forget Him again. I have finally realized that I love God and I love you, too, Nia Brooks, and I don't care who knows it."

Her brother's confessions of love shocked Raven to the core. It wasn't just his love for this woman that shocked her but his confession of love for God. She had felt that way about God for most of her life, but she'd gone off to Washington and had forgotten her first love. Raven had no clue how she would ever get that feeling back in her life, but she wanted it, more than anything.

She went over to Nia and introduced herself, "Hi, I'm Raven, Ronny's sister."

Nia hugged her. "It's so nice to finally meet you. Ronny talks about his family so much I feel as if I already know you."

Raven smiled, but inwardly she was wondering what Nia's secret was. How had she been able to get a man like Ronny to fall in love with her. Nia was beautiful, anyone could see that, but Raven had been told on countless occasions how beautiful she was, and yet, no man had ever fallen all over himself to love her. Maybe, instead of asking Nia, she should ask her sisters. Each of them had someone to love, but all Raven had was her career. But now she had the baby that was growing inside of her. Raven decided that she would love her baby and let that be enough.

***

"You can run, Raven Thomas, but you'll never be able to hide from me for long," Marcus Allen declared to the four winds as he stood on the balcony of his four thousand square foot condo.

"There you are. I've searched just about every room for you."

Inwardly groaning at the thought of having another conversation with his father's trophy wife, Marcus turned around to face off with mommy dearest. "How many copies of my house key did you make?"

"As many as I need," Liza Allen said while twirling her key ring in her hand. "Everything you do is important to this family and your father wants me to ensure that you marry well. So, we aren't going to leave you alone until you make up your mind to do the right thing."

"And what would be the right thing by your standards?" Marcus was more than fed up with this conversation. His high society step-mother thought every woman he'd ever come in contact with was beneath him. She, alone, knew who would be the perfect wife for him, at least that's what the grand Liza Allen thought. He brushed past her shaking his head.

"Allowing yourself to be photographed with that drug addicted Hartman girl sure isn't the right thing or the right image we need to project to the public."

He swung around. "Britney is a friend. And you will not disparage her in my presence. You have no idea the things she has gone through."

"We all have troubles, Marcus. But the strong don't turn to drugs as a cure for what ails them."

"You're just all heart, mommy-dearest," he said, in reference to the movie that depicted an outwardly dotting mother who secretly beat her adopted child with hangers. "And anyway, I would have thought you'd love that I was photographed with Britney. She has the right pedigree, after all... her mom is a judge."

"Britney would never survive the campaign trail. And I've told you countless times not to call me mommy-dearest."

He was tiring of this conversation. Sighing deeply, Marcus asked, "What do you want, Liza?"

"Lower your voice," she half whispered as she pointed downward. "My sorority sister and her daughter Denise Johnson are in town this weekend. I brought them over here to meet you. I thought you could show Denise around town tonight."

Marcus could feel a headache coming on. The kind of headache that shot off rockets inside his head, blinding him and rendering him useless for several hours. He'd been having these headaches ever since he was twelve and his father brought Cruella de Vil home to be his new mommy.

"Not another headache." Liza rolled her eyes as she opened her purse and pulled out a pill bottle. She handed

Marcus two pills and then opened the small refrigerator in his home office to get a bottle of water.

Marcus had one hand on his desk and the other massaging his temples. This was the one thing that he had no control over. When these headaches came, he could do nothing but ride them out and endure the pain. He took the pain pills and the water bottle offered by his step-mother, then sat down and quickly swallowed them.

"JFK had his back problems to contend with and I guess your staff at the White House will just have to work around these headaches of yours."

If his head didn't hurt so bad, Marcus would have laughed as if he were being entertained by a clown. "I hardly think it's time for you to be picking out curtains for your room in the White House. I have a long way to go before I'm ready to run for that office." Yes, Marcus was ambitious and yes, he and his father had planned his presidency since his was a kid. And even though Marcus lusted after that office as any political figure would, he was in no rush for the job.

It had become the new trend for men to aspire to the office of President of the United States of America while in their forties. But Marcus wasn't interested in greying before his time. He could wait until his late fifties, early sixties for that job.

"It's coming faster than you think. Governor Lewis will be stepping down from his office this week. He suddenly recognizes his need to spend more time with his family... that is, if they'll have him after all the catting around he's been doing."

Even with his head pounding, Marcus couldn't take this news sitting down. Pounding on his desk as he stood and declared, "You and my father made working with Governor Lewis a nightmare. I was never able to form any kind of working relationship with the man because he thought I was looking to take his place. And now you've done it." Glaring at her, he said, "I should just quit as soon as the governor resigns. Then all your meddling will have been for nothing."

Liza laughed in Marcus' face. "You won't quit. You want this just as bad as the Senator and I want it for you. And don't blame me for what's happened to Governor Lewis. Because if you had simply married like your father and I asked three years ago, you would have run for governor and with your father's endorsement, you would already be in this office and we wouldn't have had to put you in it through the backdoor. So, blame yourself for this one."

"Leave me alone; just go away." Marcus flopped back into his seat wondering why his father married a woman who was so different from his sainted mother. His mother and Liza had been friends when he was a child. They attended church together and all sorts of social events. The only difference had been that Marcus' mother was kind hearted and a God fearing woman. She had loved God and her family.

Shavona Allen had doted on him and his father. She'd taught him that doing the right thing didn't always come naturally, but if he would turn to God in prayer, God would help him find a way to do what was right. He'd forgotten a lot of things about his mother since her untimely death when he was only eleven. But he'd never forget those words. He hadn't always succeeded in doing what was right, but he'd tried his best.

"I can't leave you alone. Not when the most recent picture of you out on the town was with a drug addict."

"Okay," Marcus said calmly. "If I take this Denise... whoever out to lunch, and allow you to call up your sleazy photographers for a so-called surprise photo of me and my new lady love out on the town, then will you leave me alone?"

"You got it." She lifted her hand as if testifying before a jury. "I'll leave you alone."

As she said those words, Marcus remembered that he already had plans for this weekend. He was going to be in hot pursuit of Raven Thomas. And he was going to get answers to every question he had. Before his step-mother ran gleefully out of his home office he said, "I need an entire week. I don't want to hear from you. I don't want any of your goons spying on me... I want to be completely left alone. Got it?"

"Will you come downstairs now, Marcus, or do I need to bring the young lady up here to see you?"

"I'm not moving until we have an agreement."

Folding her arms around her chest, Liza said, "I don't like it, but if you'll go on a date with Denise and really give her a chance, I'll do it."

"Thank you. I doubt if I'll enjoy a date with a daughter of one of your stuck-up friends, but I'm going to enjoy being left alone."

"Marcus you need to understand that you are our golden boy. This family is counting on you. We have too much riding on your success to allow you to mess it up in any way."

Sometimes Marcus felt less like the golden boy and more like a trained monkey. But not this week, because

24

after today, he was going where he wanted, doing what he wanted to do and finding out all he needed to know about Raven's pregnancy, whether anyone liked it or not.

# Chapter 3

"Why are you still here, Raven? I know you have tons of work waiting for you back in D.C. Sitting at my bedside isn't going to win you any new clients," Ronny told his sister. After only four days in the hospital, they had thrown him out. But Ronny wasn't complaining. He was recuperating at his parents' home. Nia, Carmella and Raven were taking care of him and seeing that his every need was met.

"I can't leave until I know that you are all right. I would feel awful if something happened to you and I wasn't here."

"Where is your faith, little sis? God's got me. And so does Mama-Carmella and Nia. I will be okay." He then gave her a look that said he knew what she was up to. "Does this extended stay have anything to do with that Senator, the one who kept bothering you and couldn't seem to take no for an answer while we were at lunch a few weeks ago?"

"I wondered how long it would take you to ask me about Senator Allen."

Nia peeked into his room. "Hey, just checking to see if you're ready to eat."

Ronny's eyes brightened as he turned toward his lady love. "Not now, baby."

Mama-Carmella yelled from the kitchen, "Ask him if he needs a pain pill."

"Are you in pain, honey?" Nia stepped into the room and adjusted Ronny's pillow and then pulled the covers up on him.

"I can wait for about an hour on both."

"You sure, 'cause I can get you something if you need it," Nia told him.

Ronny pulled Nia's hand to his lips and kissed it. "Don't worry about me. You and Mama-Carmella have enough work to do. I'm good just sitting here with Raven for now."

"Okay, okay. I'll get out of the way." Nia walked to the bedroom door. Before leaving she told him, "But don't think you've gotten rid of me so easily, Mister. I will be back in here with food and your pain pills in one hour on the dot."

Raven burst out laughing as Nia closed the door. "You need me here to get the pillow off your head because Nia and Mama-Carmella are straight smothering you."

"What I need is for you to tell me what you've gotten yourself into. I don't like the way that senator was pushing up on you. Not to mention that he's at least Daddy's age and married."

Lifting a hand, Raven cut Ronny off. "You're right. I have gotten myself into a situation, but it's not what you think."

"Well, I'm here if you want to talk about it."

She patted him on the shoulder as she stood up. "I know. And I thank you for being a wonderful big brother. But I need to think a few things through before I can confide in anyone."

"My sister, always the professional, even when she is her own client."

Yawning, Raven told him, "I'll sit with you again this evening. I need a nap."

In her room, Raven turned on CNN as she plopped down on her bed. She doubted that she would catch much of the news because her eyelids were getting heavy and all she wanted to do was put her head on that pillow and drift off to sleep. She'd been taking a lot of power naps lately. After taking the pregnancy test, it all made sense to her. The baby was zapping her energy.

Just what she needed, Raven thought, a baby zapping all her strength while she was hiding from the father and the drama of being connected with his family. With her arms outstretched while yawning, Raven caught a glimpse of the television. Governor Lewis was having a press conference. She grabbed the remote and turned up the volume.

Governor Lewis was saying... "My family has endured many hardships because of my choice to become governor of this great state of Virginia. They have given up so much for me that I think it's only right that I now give up the governorship for them. With our children getting older and the fact that my wife and I aren't getting any younger," he smiled at his own joke, "I have decided to step down.

There is a year left to my term and I don't want this state to worry about anything. I am leaving you in good hands. Because our current lieutenant governor, Marcus Allen will be taking over and making sure that this state meets every objective we laid out during the campaign."

The anchor then went to a split screen showing Marcus Allen out to dinner with a woman who was quite beautiful but looked as if the world owed her the sun, moon and all its stars.

The anchor said, "As if he hasn't got a care in the world, the new governor was spotted in Richmond with his lady love. Ms. Denise Johnson is a socialite, who handles the Give Hope foundation for her family. From the reports we're getting in, a wedding is on the horizon."

"Oh my God, it's happening," Raven said as she put her hand on her belly. "And we're as good as dead."

*\*\**

Raven walked around the house with fear in her heart over the newscast she had witnessed the day before. Senator Allen had won re-election on a gay rights platform. According to the senator, the members of the gay community were still considered second class citizens and he wasn't going to be satisfied until they were accepted for who they were in every walk of life.

Raven remembered telling Senator Allen that he'd have to exile God and ban the Bible for that campaign promise to be fulfilled. He'd told her that all he needed was to get his son elected President of the United States and then he would unfold his plan. He'd also told her that once his plan was put in place it would be the Christians who'd have to hide who they were, "Let them see how it feels to live in the closet," he'd said with a sinister laugh.

After that conversation, she had stopped working with Senator Allen, but she had continued seeing Marcus. Why she hadn't run from the Allen family as if their house were on fire she didn't know. But if she could have gone back and prayed about any decision in her life it would have been the decision to get involved with the Allens.

"You look like a happy camper this morning," Carmella said as Raven drug herself into the kitchen.

"Just got a lot on my mind, is all."

"You want to talk?"

Raven shook her head. "I don't want to make you late for church."

Carmella handed Raven a banana. "Come with me and then I'll take you to lunch after church so we can talk."

Raven peeled the banana and took a bite. She was about ready to fix her mouth to make her excuses, but then the banana did the backstroke in her stomach and made its way back up. Raven clamped her hand over her mouth and ran to the bathroom. Hugging the toilet, she spilled her guts into it and then dry heaved until her stomach calmed down.

Carmella rubbed her back. "Are you okay?" she asked as Raven let go of the toilet and leaned against the wall.

"How old was that banana?" Raven asked, trying to act as if she were just as surprised as Carmella by her violent reaction to a simple banana.

"I just picked those up at the grocery yesterday. I'm so sorry, honey. I never would have given you that banana if I thought it wasn't any good."

Not wanting Carmella to feel guilty, Raven said, "It probably wasn't the banana. My stomach has been sour all night long. I guess it just erupted this morning."

Carmella held out her hand for Raven. "Go lay back down. I'll bring you the CD from this morning's service."

The look of compassion on Carmella's face caused Raven to remember what it was like when she lived in this house and the family went off to church together. She grabbed hold of Carmella's hand, stood up and told her, "I don't want the CD. I'm coming to church with you this morning. Just give me a half hour and I'll be ready."

\*\*\*

Raven kept her word and attended church with Carmella that morning. And she was fascinated when the minister started preaching about Phinehas, a story she had never even noticed in the scriptures.

"Turn in your Bibles to Numbers 25. We'll begin reading at verse 3...

*"Israel joined himself unto Baal-peor: and the anger of the Lord was kindled against Israel. And the Lord said unto Moses, take all the heads of the people, and hang them up before the Lord against the sun, that the fierce anger of the Lord may be turned away from Israel. And Moses said unto the judges of Israel, slay ye every one his men that were joined unto Baal-peor. And, behold, one of the children of Israel came and brought unto his brethren a Midianitish woman in the sight of Moses, and in the sight of all the congregation of the children of Israel, who were weeping before the door of the tabernacle of the congregation.*

*"And when Phinehas, the son of Eleazar, the son of Aaron the priest, saw it, he rose up from among the congregation, and took a javelin in his hand; and he went after the man of Israel into the tent, and thrust both of them through, the man of Israel, and the woman through her belly. So the plague was stayed from the children of Israel...*

*"And the Lord spake unto Moses, saying, Phinehas, the son of Eleazar, the son of Aaron the priest, hath turned My wrath away from the children of Israel."*

After reading the scriptures the minister said, "In case you weren't able to follow the reading of the Word, let me break it down for you. The nation of Israel had sinned by worshiping an idol named Baal-Peor. One sin led to another and as I read in the text, the Israelites became so bold in their sin that one of them brought a Midianitish woman, in today's language, a prostitute, to another Israelite so he could lay with her. He did this in front of Moses and anyone else who was looking.

"The people recognized sin when they saw it, knew that this thing displeased God, but all they did was weep about it. But Phinehas had had enough. By this time, the sins they were committing had brought a plague on the nation... have you heard of a few things like AIDS, herpes, syphilis, gonorrhea... these are all sexually transmitted diseases (plagues) that come from us deciding that we can do whatever we want, live any way we want and no one can tell us any different."

As the preacher continued ministering about sexual immorality in such a bold fashion that Raven hadn't heard in a long time, her hand swept across her belly. She felt guilty of the sin this man spoke of and could have very well contracted one of the diseases he'd just outlined, instead of the baby that was now growing in her body. "God forgive me," she whispered to the God she had tried to put out of her mind the last few years that she'd been working in D.C. But God had never let go of her, that's why she still had the ability to feel such guilt over sleeping with a man who wasn't her husband.

When service was over Raven went to the minister and shook his hand. "I was supposed to be here today. Thank you for preaching the word of God and not being afraid to tell the truth."

"We have to speak out, my dear sister. Because we are losing believers to the enemy right and left. Some of them are so deep into their immoralities that we may never get them back. My prayer is that by lifting up my voice, I can save at least one person from going down the wrong path then I will feel as if I've done some good with this life God gave me."

As Raven walked away from the minister, she was struck by how much it meant to him that he used his life in service to God. When she first began her work in political public relations, all she'd wanted was to do some good for mankind, but then she decided that maybe the best way to do good for mankind was by first doing what was good and right for God.

"Thank you for coming to church with me today," Carmella said as they sat down at the table preparing to order their breakfast.

"I'm glad you invited me. I have never heard anyone preach on this Phinehas person. It was fascinating and gave me a great deal to think about."

"God has a way of getting our attention when we least expect it. I'm glad you're listening. Now, do me a favor and let God lead you wherever He desires to take you."

Getting defensive, Raven said, "You think I went against God when I decided on my career, don't you?"

Shaking her head, Carmella told her, "I didn't say that. I can't say that, because I don't know what God's purpose is for you. All I'm asking is that you allow God to reveal it to you."

They ordered their food and then Raven took a deep breath and said, "I need to tell you something. I don't want you to freak out or to tell Daddy before I'm ready."

Carmella put her hand over Raven's. "You can tell me anything. You know that. But I have to be honest with you, your father doesn't like for me to keep secrets, so I can't guarantee anything on that front. Can you live with that?"

Before Raven could answer, her cell phone rang. Looking down at the caller ID she saw that it was Joe. "I have to take this," she told Carmella as she excused herself from the table. Once she was outside of the restaurant she answered and asked, "Did you find her?"

Raven had left town, but she wasn't neglecting her duties to her firm. Joe hired a private detective to find Britney's location and now she was hoping to hear some good news.

"I had a bead on her, but Marcus must have known we were coming, because she was relocated last night. But the good news is that Britney is still alive. I showed her picture to several residents of the rehab center where she was supposed to be and they remembered her."

"Well thank God for small favors. But what am I supposed to tell Britney's mother?"

"Tell her that Britney is safe and getting the help she needs."

She heard the voice, but hoped and prayed that her ears were deceiving her. Raven slowly turned around and came face to face with the man she both loved and feared.

# Chapter 4

"What are you doing here? Are you following me?" Raven was practically screaming.

"Who is it?" Joe asked.

Raven was still holding the cell to her ear. She quickly answered. "Governor Marcus Allen is standing in front of me. I'll call you back later." She hung up the phone and wrapped her arms around her chest as she glared at him.

"I'm happy to see you, too," Marcus said in a manner that indicated the opposite.

"If you don't want to be in my presence, why on earth did you follow me?"

"You know why I'm here. And please don't think you'll be able to double talk your way out of this. I want answers and I want them now."

"I don't owe you anything."

"I disagree." He pointed at her belly. "Is it mine or not?"

Caught off guard by his bold question and then angered by his assumption that someone else could be the father of the baby she was carrying, Raven started yelling at him. "How dare you follow me all the way to my hometown to accuse me of sleeping around. I leave all the cheating to you and  ex-Governor Lewis, who suddenly remembered he had a family that needs him."

"Hey, don't try to put Governor Lewis' problem on me. I don't have a wife and if I did, she wouldn't have to worry about infidelity."

"Mmph, sure. You're just the model of fidelity, just like your daddy."

"What's that supposed to mean?"

"It means that I saw you on the news with Denise Johnson, your fiancée. Remember her?" When she said the word fiancée, she put her fingers in the air and imitated quotation marks.

"I'm not engaged to anyone, yet. And I'm not involved with Denise, either. I hope you believe me."

"Of course I believe you. You Allen men are born truth tellers." She leaned back, studied him, and then hit him with, "Tell me, Marcus, have they ever found that woman who claimed that the senator was the father of her baby?"

"I don't have anything to do with that, either."

"Don't you?" Raven was outraged that this man would come after her like she had no connections and could be disposed of as easily as the beauty queen his father had the affair with. "Your father sent you here to take care of me, didn't he? I know how Senator Allen thinks. Now that you're the acting governor, he's not going to want anything in the way of you winning the next election."

"Nothing will be in the way."

"I don't care how powerful your family is, I will not have an abortion. I never intended to get pregnant, but now that it's happened, I will just deal with it."

"You mean, *we* will deal with it… right?" The look he gave dared her to challenge his rights as they related to a child of his.

Leaning back and looking up at him she said, "All right then, Governor, what do you suggest we do about this?"

"I thought you'd never ask… it's simple. We call a press conference, announce our engagement and then do a quickie wedding."

The wind was knocked out of Raven. Had she heard him right? No man had ever asked her to marry him. She'd been the bridesmaid for both her sisters and a few friends. She'd imagined that she'd have to be content with her career, because she didn't have anyone in her life… and then she'd met Marcus.

Her eyes traveled the distance as she gazed up at him. At six feet five inches, he was a whole foot taller than her. At one point in their wayward romance, she had enjoyed looking up at him. His height and solid build put her in the mind of that old fable, John Henry, the hammer wielding man. Being born with a silver spoon in his mouth, Marcus never had to do such menial tasks, but the way he was built, he could do more than wield a hammer, if need be.

*Snap out of it*, she told herself. *Every woman in Virginia knows how fine Marcus Allen is.* She wasn't the first woman to crush on him and she certainly wouldn't be the last. "I can't marry you," she snapped her fingers, "just like that."

"Why not? If it's my baby you're carrying, I would think you'd welcome marriage."

Raven glanced around. They were standing outside the restaurant and she prayed that no one heard Marcus' loud mouth. "Can you keep it down?"

"Oh, am I too loud for you?" He glanced around just as she had done. "What? You don't want anyone in your hometown to know about me?"

"*You* shouldn't want them to know, Governor," she said, trying to remind him of who he was and all that should mean to him. "And besides, who said I'm pregnant by you, anyway?"

He laughed at her. "If you're pregnant, then the baby is mine. I know that for a fact. I only asked it if was mine to mess with you, because I'm still angry that you left without talking to me."

"How come you're so confident?"

He didn't answer.

Raven's eyes widened as she realized… "You had me followed?"

"Not me. But let's just say there's a reason why my father is up in arms about your pregnancy."

"Your father is the devil. I should have known he was having me followed." She lifted her cell phone and punched in Joe's number. When he answered she said, "Can you have my apartment swept again?" They swept their places once a quarter. With the type of work they did and the high profile clients they had, Raven liked to ensure that her clients' information would be kept confidential, no matter where it was discussed. But the last sweep had occurred over three months ago... time for another one.

"I'll get it done tonight. Why don't you ask the governor where he stashed Britney?" Joe said before hanging up.

Putting her phone back in her purse, she did exactly what Joe suggested. "Judge Hartman wants her daughter back home. What did you do with her?"

Marcus shook his head. "Sometimes I wonder why you even slept with me, because you obviously have a very low opinion of me."

When Raven didn't respond, Marcus said, "Relax, tell the judge that Britney is somewhere safe and very discreet. No one will leak her whereabouts or her condition to the press. So, her election should go off without a hitch."

"I'm sure that Judge Hartman is worried about more than just her re-election."

Laughing, Marcus said, "Please... she might be holy and sanctified these days, but she still bleeds red, white and blue, just like my family."

Raven opened her mouth to tell Marcus just what she thought of his family and their privileged attitude, but the restaurant door opened and Carmella came out. "Hey, what's taking you so long? Your food is getting cold."

Raven outwardly groaned. The last thing she wanted was for Mama-Carmella and Marcus to come face to face. The Allens would do anything to get what they wanted, and Raven feared that Marcus might harm a member of her family just to get at her. Actually, if she was telling herself the truth, she didn't fear what Marcus would do, and didn't believe that he would harm her family, but his father was another story. She didn't want Senator Allen knowing anything about her family, and therefore, she needed to keep Marcus' nose out of her family's business.

"I'll be right there, just go back inside, okay?" Raven implored Carmella.

Carmella gave her a strange look but turned and went back inside.

Raven then tried to walk away from Marcus but he grabbed hold of her arm. "We're not done."

"Oh yes we are," she told him as she pulled her arm out of his grasp. "Don't come near me. Just stay away."

"I'm not about to leave you alone until we settle this matter between us. I'll come to your parents' home if I have to. Is that what you want... for me to come to your parents' house and give them a blow by blow of what we've been up to?"

"I am telling my family myself this weekend. I don't need you running your mouth about anything that concerns me."

"Then you need to make time for me."

"All right, all right. I'll meet you later tonight. I'll text you with the location."

"You better show up tonight, or you'll regret it."

"I already do," Raven told him as she opened the restaurant door and left him to watch her walk away.

*** 

Raven plopped down on the couch in her parents' family room. Marcus had tracked her to her hometown and that was just too close for comfort. She didn't want them involved with any member of the Allen family. When the Allens got involved, people came up missing.

She needed to find out where Marcus was hiding Britney, so she was going to keep her meeting with him tonight, but she didn't want to come up missing or have anything happen to her family, so she was going to leave Raleigh first thing in the morning.

"You look like there's a million things on your mind," Carmella said as she walked into the room and sat down next to her.

Sighing, Raven said, "Yeah, I need to get back to work."

"Somehow I don't think it's work that's on your mind."

Why she ever thought she could fool Mama-Carmella, Raven didn't know. It was as if the woman had a direct line to God and He fed her information about the family on a daily basis.

"Does what you're worried about have anything to do with what you wanted to talk to me about at breakfast before you took that call?"

No sense in lying, God had probably already told Mama-Carmella to start knitting some baby booties. "Can we go up to my room?"

Carmella stood. "Lead the way."

When they were in her room with the door closed, Raven thought that confessing her misdeeds would be easier. After all, she was a fully grown woman with a business of her own. She was living away from her parents and paying her own bills. But right now she felt as if she were about to confess that she'd been caught up in a bribery scheme and the feds were about to bust down the door and arrest her... she felt like coming back home pregnant without a husband was just as shameful as being a corrupt politician.

Her mouth felt as if it were holding molasses because she couldn't open it. Raven Thomas, the girl who didn't just run a business, but one in the heart of D.C. politics and could stand toe to toe with the best of them, was now afraid of what her mommy would say about her pregnancy.

Sitting down next to Raven, Carmella began rubbing her back. "Who was that man you were talking to earlier?"

Tears began forming in Raven's eyes. Sighing deeply, she said, "His name is Marcus Allen. His father is Senator Allen."

Carmella looked away for a moment, then snapped her fingers. "I just saw something about him on CNN. They've been looking for him to get a statement. That man just became acting governor of his state and he's down here chasing behind you? What's going on, Raven? You know you can tell me anything, so I don't understand why you're hesitating."

Wiping the tears from her face, Raven put her big girl pants on and blurted out, "I'm pregnant."

Carmella's hand went to her mouth. When she uncovered it she said, "I think I knew that already."

"What?"

"Of course," Carmella said. "You've been so tired and then the throwing up... your dad asked me if I thought you should see a doctor and to tell you the truth, at that moment I thought to myself... she doesn't have anything that nine months won't cure."

"Why didn't you say anything? I've been torturing myself, trying to figure out a way to break this news to all of you." Raven shook her head. "I should have known that God had revealed it to you. So do you already know what else I'm dealing with?"

"I can't put that one on God. I've been pregnant twice and watched all of Joy's and your sisters-in-law carry their babies. I thought I knew, but I wasn't sure."

Putting a pillow in her lap, Raven said, "Still, I wish you had said something to me."

"You're a grown woman, Raven. I don't think it's our place to pry into your and your brothers' and sisters' lives. Ramsey and I just pray for each of you and trust that God is able to see you all through anything that comes your way."

"Well God must have been asleep on this one, because I've gotten myself involved in something that I can't see a clear way out of."

"Is the new governor the father?" Carmella asked with no judgment in her voice.

Raven nodded. "I messed up big time."

"Why was the governor here? Is he trying to get you to hide the fact that the baby is his?"

"His father would rather me and my baby be aborted than the political aspirations he has for his son be halted. But Marcus wants to call a press conference and announce our engagement and then do a quickie marriage."

"So what's the problem?" Carmella asked, looking confused. "You do love him, don't you?"

"I think I fell in love with Marcus the week after we met. But that in itself is the problem. Since everything happened so fast, I had no clue just how evil his father is and no idea of the plans that he has for Marcus." Shaking her head, Raven told Carmella, "I just can't be a part of that."

"Well," Carmella exhaled. "All I can tell you to do is to pray real hard. Marriage is serious business, and you would be joining yourself to their family. You need to figure out if you're ready for that."

"I can't believe that you're not screaming at me, or pounding me over the head with the Bible. I'm thirty years old and I was still afraid to come home and tell you that I am pregnant."

Carmella put her arms around Raven and hugged her. "I don't have any stones to throw at you. And neither will your father, I guarantee you that. You were raised right, so I truly believe that even though you've made a mistake, if you put it in God's hands, He'll turn it around and make it work out for your good and His glory. Who knows, you might be carrying a future president in your belly. One that will call the people back to holiness instead of all this ungodly stuff that we are enduring now."

# Chapter 5

"I didn't think you were going to show up," Marcus said as he greeted Raven.

"I reserved this room, why wouldn't I show up." After talking things over with Mama-Carmella, Raven contacted a restaurateur she knew in the area and arranged to rent out his private dining area. She was, after all, meeting with a very new governor, discussing some delicate matters.

"As usual, your public relations expertise is paying off." He pointed towards a buffet table that was lined with fruits, vegetables and chicken and steak. Pitchers of water and iced tea were already at their table. "You thought of everything."

"I didn't want to take the chance of anyone coming in and out of the room and taking pictures or filming us."

"Like I said, you thought of everything. My father would be pleased. But I guess that's why he hired you in the first place."

Grabbing a plate and beginning to fill it, Raven said, "Your father is no longer a client of mine and you know that."

Following suit, Marcus picked up a plate and said, "Yes, but I still don't understand why you dropped me at the same time you dropped my father from your client roster."

As they sat down across from each other, Raven put her cards on the table. "Okay, I was wrong for not communicating with you concerning my reasons for ending our relationship."

"Finally, she admits it."

Putting her fork down, Raven glared at him. "Are you going to be obnoxious or are you going to let me finish."

Lifting his hands, he leaned back. "You have the floor. Please, enlighten me."

"The thing is," she began, "our families are very different. My parents believe in traditional family values, morality and God's absolute right to dictate what morality is. But your parents seem to believe anything goes and sway whichever way the polls go. I couldn't subject a child of mine to that."

"What's so horrible about being a part of my family?" He held up a hand. "Okay, I know something happened between you and my father, but that doesn't mean he's not a good guy. And don't ask me to feel some type of way about being his son, because I'm grateful that Senator Michael Allen is my father. I certainly wouldn't be where I am today if not for him."

"But where are you?" Raven leaned forward as she said, "My dad used to tell me that if a man didn't have God, he didn't have much."

"And what makes you think that we don't have God?" Marcus asked. His tone indicated that he was very offended by her comment. "Before my mom died we all attended church twice a week. My family loved God and my mom wanted nothing more than to please Him. But after she died so suddenly, I guess we just fell off of our routine and then my dad married Liza. I was only twelve when they married and I was at the age where I didn't want to sit in church for hours on end anymore, so it didn't bother me that Liza never attended church, but I will admit that as I got older I began to miss it. My pastor said that I was drawn back to church because my mother raised me to appreciate the presence of God, so don't tell me about my morals and values."

She wanted to ask why he had slept with her if he was so moral and wanting to please God, but then she would have to answer the same question.

"I'm not perfect, Raven. I don't attend church as much as I should, and I've been so busy working that I haven't even thought about Bible study lately. But no matter what you think, I do love God and would support your need to instill Christian values in our child."

Well, the boy just said a mouthful. Raven had nothing else to do but to admit, "Your father told me about your mother. She was the reason I took him on as a client." She didn't add that she'd later found his father and step-mother to be frauds. Raven had never told Marcus about that last conversation she'd had with his father while she was still working for the man.

Raven believed in holding the confidence of her clients, even the ones she totally disagreed with, so she couldn't even warn Marcus about what his father was up to. Since Marcus would soon be the father of her child, all Raven could hope was that Marcus would be able to stand against all the demonic forces that were sure to be coming at him. Then she had a thought... wouldn't the father of her child be able to stand against his parents' ungodly crusade even better if she was by his side?

"So, you really don't want me to have an abortion?"

Putting his napkin down, Marcus said, "Raven, I have a pro-life platform, that's non-negotiable for me. I believe every life is important and especially any life I had anything to do with creating."

"And you were serious when you asked me to marry you?"

"As serious as a governor in need of a wife."

"Now we get to it. The only reason you want to marry me is to keep that governor's title. How romantic."

Raven was shaking her head as Marcus put his hands over hers. "I'm not going to lie to you, hon. Having a baby without being married could derail my next campaign. But I wouldn't marry you just for political reasons. I felt something when we were together. I believe I could love you, if you'd just give me the chance."

His words felt honest and pure. Although she had fallen for him the week after they met, Raven was grateful that he didn't claim to be head over heels in love because she would have thought he was lying. A man like Marcus who could have any woman he wanted wouldn't just fall all over himself for a girl like her. She was the always-a-bridesmaid-never-a-bride kind of girl. Now she felt like the most popular boy in school was asking her to the prom.

Things like this didn't happen to Raven... they happened to her younger sister, Renee, who had walked down the aisle two years ago. Raven, of course, had been Renee's bridesmaid. Just once, she'd like for someone to be her bridesmaid and take unreasonable requests from her. Could this work between her and Marcus? "I'm just not sure if your family would allow us to be a family. I don't agree with anything your father stands for."

"Despite what you think, my father doesn't run my life. I know what I want, and it's you... you and my baby. So, what do you say? Is it going to be marriage or single parenthood for the both of us?"

Single parenthood didn't sound like much fun, but neither did coming up missing, as the women in the Allen circle tended to do. Unless her radar was completely off, Raven didn't believe that Marcus had anything to do with the disappearance of his father's mistress. But she also wanted to make sure that Britney was okay before she said 'I do'.

"I have two requests."

"For the future Mrs. Allen, ask whatever you want. I can't move heaven, but I can sure enough shake this earth until it releases your heart's desire."

See, this was why she'd lost her head and slept with a man she wasn't married to. Marcus opened his mouth and her knees buckled. The man was too smooth for his own good. Ignoring the butterflies in her stomach, she said, "The first thing I need is for you to come back to the house and talk to my parents with me."

"Done. What else?"

"I need you to take me to Britney. I promised her mother that I would find her daughter. I at least need to be able to tell Judge Hartman that Britney is okay."

He leaned back in his seat. Stared at her for a moment, then asked, "Non-negotiable?"

She nodded, "Non-negotiable."

Clasping his hands together, he said, "I'll tell you what. You do this press conference with me so that we can announce our engagement and then I'll take you to see Britney."

"Why can't we go see Britney first?"

"I have to be back home in the morning for a press conference that's already been scheduled. I'm the new governor, remember?"

"How could I forget?" She took a sip of water.

"So, I figured I could bring you to the press conference with me. Since this is my first press conference as governor, it would be the perfect time to also announce my engagement. I doubt that we'll have very many people wondering about why we decided to get engaged if we bunch everything into one press conference."

Made sense to her. "Okay, but I don't want your parents knowing anything about our engagement until after we make the announcement."

He held out his hand. "Deal." They shook on it and then left the restaurant to go and take care of Raven's first request.

\*\*\*

"Are you sure about this?" Carmella asked as she, Raven and Nia sat in the family room, while Ramsey and Marcus were discussing this marriage and baby thing in the study.

"I think so. I mean, it's better than being a single mom."

"I did that for several years and let me tell you, I am thrilled to be engaged to your brother," Nia admitted. "He is the love of my life and I no longer have to do everything myself."

Carmella chimed in. "After my first husband divorced me and left me with one grown child and another to finish raising on my own, I was scared because I had never had all of the parenting responsibility on me. But I didn't marry your father just so I wouldn't have to do it on my own," Carmella told Raven.

"That's not what I meant," Nia said quickly. "I love Ronny. He is perfect for me or I wouldn't be marrying him."

"I'm not worried about you and Ronny," Carmella told her. "I know the two of you are in love." She then turned to Raven and asked, "What about you. Do you love this man?"

Raven didn't want to seem pathetic, admitting to loving a man who, at best, liked her a lot. So she said, "If I didn't have feelings for him, I never would have slept with him. But this marriage is more about becoming a family so that we both can raise our child and Marcus can continue to have the political career he's worked so hard to build."

Carmella sat down next to Raven, put her arm around her shoulder. "But I want so much more for you."

"It's not just me that I have to think about anymore. Marcus will make a good father. He makes me laughed and I lo…" she hesitated as she almost said the word 'love', "enjoy being around him."

"If this is what you want…" Carmella's voice gave way to the worry she felt in her gut.

"It's what I want, Mama-Carmella, so be happy for me." She squeezed Carmella's hand. "And besides, if I don't marry Marcus and his father gets his hooks in my child, I'd never forgive myself."

"The truth of the matter is, you won't be able to stop his family from getting their hooks into your child no matter what," Nia said and then added, "I thought that not mentioning Jarod's grandparents would make them go away. But Jarod was always thinking about them, even when I wasn't. If Ronny hadn't talked them into seeing my son, I don't know what I would have done. But I know Jarod would still feel as if he were missing a part of himself."

"I'm okay with my child knowing his grandparents. I just don't want them having too much influence in his or her life. I know Senator Allen personally, and let's just say, I wouldn't vote for him."

"Let me ask you something, Raven," Carmella said as she leaned forward and looked her directly in the eye. "How's your prayer life?"

Silence fell over the room. Raven was ashamed to admit that since leaving home and starting her business, she hadn't had much of a prayer life at all. But Raven was confident that Mama-Carmella already knew the answer to her question, so she said, "Truthfully, I haven't prayed much, nor have I read my Bible as much as I should have since my business took over my life."

"Then might I suggest that you begin to include God in your family, and whatever outcome you want for Marcus and your unborn child, pray and ask God for it."

# Chapter 6

First thing Monday morning Marcus and Raven went to the courthouse and applied for their marriage license. It was now 11 a.m. and Marcus was standing in front of a bunch of clambering reporters looking dapper and ready for business in his dark blue double breasted suit.

The first reporter said to him, "How does it feel to be governor without having to go through a grueling campaign?"

"I don't know about that. My friend, ex-governor Lewis only had a year left to his term, so I'll have to work really hard in the next few months if I want to be elected for another term."

"What's your first order of business?" Another reporter asked.

Marcus showed off that dimpled grin that never ceased to make Raven weak in the knees and then he said in a self-deprecating way, "Relax everyone, this is my first day on the job. Allow me a few days to get up to speed and then I'll be able to make a few educated decisions."

Raven was grinning like a fool in love. Marcus hadn't received his talking points from her and yet he was answering every question just right.

A reporter in the back of the room called out, "Why weren't you available for comment this weekend? Didn't you know that the former governor would be resigning?"

For that question, Marcus turned adoring eyes on Raven. He put his hand in hers and pulled her closer. He then turned back to the reporters and said, "I didn't know about Governor Lewis' announcement until the last minute and I had already planned to be with my fiancée and her family this weekend. We were busy with the final details of our wedding, so my absence couldn't be helped." Marcus then lifted Raven's hand to his lips and kissed the back of it.

Raven's knees buckled as she looked into Marcus' eyes. She had to remind herself that he was just playing up to the cameras and was not really in love with her as anyone would believe from the look on his face.

"Ladies and gentlemen," Marcus said as he turned back to the reporters, "meet my bride-to-be, Ms. Raven Thomas."

"What happened to Denise, Marcus? Weren't you just on a date with her last week?" One of the reporters called out.

"Denise Johnson and I are just friends. Are families have none each other for years. But there's no love connection there. You all just snapped the wrong photo is all."

All Raven's years of training in public relations hadn't prepared Raven for what to do when the cameras were turned onto her. Marcus was handling himself expertly, but with the goofy expression on her face, all she could do was wave to the group as if she were Miss America, walking the runway with a diamond studded crown on her head.

"How long have you been engaged to the governor?"

"How did you get him to propose, Ms. Thomas?"

The questions kept coming until Marcus raised his hand. "Hey, no badgering my lady. She might reconsider marrying me and then I'd be a very unhappy governor."

Laughs went around the room and then Marcus expertly fielded a few more questions and then called the press conference to a close. As they were headed back to his office Raven reminded him, "It's time for you to take me to see Britney."

"Okay, let me stop in the office for a little bit and then we'll take care of that," Marcus promised her.

But when they arrived at the governor's office, Senator Allen was seated in his office waiting for them with the city's most high profile judge. "I didn't know you were in town," Marcus said as he went to his father and hugged him.

"I bet you didn't. But you can't get much past your old man. I've told you that all your life, but for some reason you keep trying."

Marcus tried to keep the laugher out of his voice as he said, "We were going to tell you about the engagement, Dad. I just wanted to make the announcement at the press conference first."

"And we both know why that is, don't we?" Senator Allen patted his son on the shoulder. "But you're a grown man, so I figure that you're entitled to defy your father at least once or twice a year." He wagged a finger at Marcus and then added, "But no more than that."

Ignoring his father's comment, Marcus asked, "Why didn't you join me at the press conference?"

"This is your first day as governor. You and I always knew this day would come, and I didn't want to steal your thunder in any way, shape or form." With adoration in his eyes, the senator said, "I'm proud of you, son."

"Thanks, but we both know I wouldn't be here if it weren't for you." Marcus meant that in more ways than one, but he kept the conversation upbeat and didn't allow the expression on his face to give away any of the negative vibes he was feeling about the way in which he received the governor's office.

"And we want to make sure you keep it, at least for one more term… and then it's the White House for you. But first, we need to get you married off."

Raven got a funny feeling in the pit of her stomach. She glanced at Judge Parker and then at Marcus. When he looked her way, Raven shook her head, trying to let him know that she wasn't interested in his father's game plan.

"We've got this covered, Dad. Raven and I picked up the marriage license this morning. We're going to figure out the wedding stuff in the next few weeks."

"You don't have time to procrastinate. If you want this marriage, then it has to be now. I've invested too much in you to allow you to throw it all away just because you've got too much of a conscious to do what I told you to do in the first place."

Marcus was busy staring his father down when Raven nudged his shoulder. "What is he talking about?"

Shifting his eyes toward Raven he said, "We need to talk." He turned back to his father. "Can you and Judge Parker excuse yourselves for a moment?"

"Sure thing," Senator Allen quickly responded. "We'll just keep your assistant company. Maybe I'll give her a few assignments to get your first day started off right."

"Don't talk to my assistant," Marcus called out as his father left his office.

With her arms folded across her chest, Raven asked, "What did your father want you to do, that you didn't?"

"I'm sorry about that, Raven. He shouldn't have said that in front of you."

"Don't be sorry, just tell me what he was talking about."

Marcus took Raven's hand and walked her over to the sofa and sat down with her. "I hate telling you this because I know you already have a low opinion of my father, but you have to understand that he was only thinking of what would be best for my career."

She did a hand motion, indicating that he should get on with it.

"He wanted me to ask you to have an abortion, okay? Are you happy now that you know that?"

"You don't sound very happy about it," Raven said as she noted the creases in Marcus' forehead.

"I'll admit that my father's suggestion bothered me. When he first ran for the senate over twenty years ago, it was on a family first platform. It's just hard for me to believe that a man like that could so easily discard his own grandchild." Marcus looked off into the distance as if he couldn't face Raven with the truth he now knew about his father.

"Well at least he didn't kill me, like he did with his mistress," Raven said flippantly.

Marcus did not take kindly to that remark. "That's not funny, Raven. My father may have his flaws, but he's not a killer."

"He wanted to kill my baby. What makes you think he wouldn't kill a woman who was claiming to be pregnant by him and was scheduled to do an interview with that new CNN anchor when she came up missing?"

"We're supposed to be discussing our life, not my father's, remember?"

Raven stood up and wrapped her arms around her chest. "I don't like that discussion either. I don't see why I have to get married today. I have been a bridesmaid four times already, it's time for someone to be my bridesmaid and fuss over me." She stomped her foot like a stubborn child.

Marcus pulled her into his arms, rubbing her back, he said, "I know it's not fair to you, hon. But I am a public figure and we need to make this right as soon as possible."

With pouty lips, Raven told him, "I know we have to do a quickie wedding, but I thought I had at least a month to plan it."

"The longer we wait the greater the chance that you'll start showing. We don't want anyone snapping a picture of the governor's fiancée with a baby bump, now do we?"

Reluctantly, Raven admitted that Marcus was right. "In another month I'll be three months pregnant. And I have known women who started showing that early, so I guess we do need to get married immediately."

Kissing his bride on the forehead, Marcus said, "Thank you for understanding, baby. I might not be able to give you the wedding of your dreams, but I promise that I'll do everything in my power to give you a marriage that most women only dream about having."

Stepping out of his embrace, Raven told him, "I don't know if I can trust your promises anymore."

Marcus looked wounded. "What do you mean? What have I done this early in our engagement to cause you to doubt me?"

"You promised to take me to Britney after the press conference. But instead of handling my business, I'm stuck here pacifying your father."

"I will take you to Britney this weekend. I promise."

Shaking her head, Raven told him, "That's not good enough. If you want me to say 'I do' today, then you need to let me know where Britney is and I'll send Joe to check on her." Raven pulled out her cell phone and stared at Marcus, waiting for him to provide her with the information she was demanding.

He hesitated, but only for a moment. "All right, you win, call Joe and I'll tell him where he can find Britney. But I want her left where she is. She needs time to get her life back on track."

"Deal," Raven said as she dialed Joe and then handed Marcus the phone.

When Marcus finished speaking to Joe, he handed Raven back her cell phone and then said, "Come on, it's time to get hitched."

Shaking her head as she followed Marcus out of his office, Raven said, "Here comes the bride."

# Chapter 7

"He tricked me," Raven declared, looking at the diamond on her ring finger as she held her cell phone up to her ear.

Joe said, "I didn't even know the two of you were dating. Then I turn on the news and discover that you're engaged to our very own political wonder boy."

"Life is funny sometimes," Raven said, but at the moment she didn't mean funny, ha-ha. More like the-joke-was-on-her kinda funny.

"You keep your business and your clients' business close to the vest, I can respect that. But how is this going to make us look to our client... you get engaged to the last person she knew to be with her daughter, he gives us her location, but when I get there I discover that Britney has been relocated again."

"We're not engaged anymore. We got married yesterday." Raven dreaded telling Joe that, because she was already feeling like a fool, but having others know how big of a fool she had been was something Raven could hardly stomach. But the senator had already leaked the news to the media, so the word would be out soon enough.

"But you just announced your engagement."

She could hear the puzzlement in his voice, but there was no way she was going to tell him of her pregnancy and look like an even bigger fool, just to give him clarity. "The governor's schedule is tight, this was the only time we had to get married within the next few months."

"I see."

"I'll be in to work in about an hour, we can talk further then," Raven told Joe as she hung up the phone. Something stank to high heaven and she needed to get to the bottom of it before she was pulled into the muck with the stench.

Flinging off the covers, she hopped out of the bed she had shared with her husband the night before. The man she had vowed to love, honor and cherish. But he had double crossed her, so as far as Raven was concerned, all bets were off.

As she got out of the shower she was greeted by her lying husband. He was still in his robe and grinning from ear to ear as he studied her body. Raven quickly grabbed a towel and wrapped it around herself. "I thought you had already left for the office."

He shook his head. "I went downstairs to make you some breakfast, I thought we could have breakfast in bed before getting our day started.

She didn't like the way he was looking at her, as if breakfast was the last thing on his mind, but getting her back in that bed was the first, second and third thing he was contemplating.

She brushed past him, feeling too close for comfort in the spa-like bathroom. She needed to move this conversation into the spacious bedroom. "I don't have time for breakfast, I have to get to work."

"Breakfast is the most important meal of the day, dear wife."

She closed her eyes and wrapped her arms around herself as he said the word 'wife', all the while hearing the words from that old 1970s song, Love Don't Love Nobody… It takes a fool to learn, and she was certainly Marcus Allen's fool. Pulling her form fitting dress on and then climbing into her three inch heels, Raven tried to calm herself as she turned back to her husband and demanded, "Where is she?"

He set the breakfast tray down on the bed. "Where is who?"

"You know exactly who I'm asking about." Pointing an accusatory finger in his face, she said, "You sent Joe on a wild goose chase and then walked me down the aisle as if everything was just fine, when all the while you knew that Britney was long gone from the latest rehab you stashed her in."

"What are you talking about? Britney isn't gone. She liked that place. She told me that the facility worked for her. She was taking long walks, sitting by the river and clearing her head."

"She's not there and you know it," Raven hated yelling but this man was getting on her nerves. He was a deceiver and she wasn't going to play his game any longer. She started marching towards the door.

"Wait, I'll prove it to you." Raven stopped as Marcus picked up the phone and dialed the facility. He asked to speak with the manager of the facility. When the man came on the line, Marcus said, "Hey, how are things going down there?"

"As good as can be expected," the manager told him.

"How is Britney? Is she responding well to therapy?"

"Britney's no longer here. I thought you knew that she checked herself out two days ago."

"I had no clue. I've been a little busy and didn't have time to check on her. Why did you let her check out of there? I told you she needed to be there for at least a month."

"She was a voluntary patient, we couldn't force her to stay."

Marcus hung up and then turned back to Raven. His eyes held confusion. "I didn't know. But I'll find her, I promise you that."

"I'm good on your promises. My team will find her, just stay away from me." She had run away from her responsibilities to her clients when she feared that his father would be coming after her. But she wasn't running from the Allens anymore. She'd tell the world every sordid detail she knew about this family if she had to, but one way or another she was bringing Britney back to Judge Hartman.

He grabbed her arm as she attempted to leave. "I'm on your team, remember?" He held up his ring finger. "We're married."

Snatching away from him, she said, "And now I realize that it was all politics. You couldn't care less about this baby, so get out of my way."

"I didn't do anything to Britney. I'm her friend, Raven. She came to me for help and that's what I've been doing.

I'm not trying to sabotage your investigation or anything. I honestly don't know why she checked herself out of that rehab, when she clearly needs to be there."

She was done listening to him. "I'm late for work." Stepping around the governor, Raven left his house, vowing never to return.

But as she was driving in to work, her cell phone rang twice. The first call came from Marcus. Raven let it go to voicemail. The second call was not so easily ignored. Mama-Carmella was calling. She had forgotten to call her family to let them know that she and Marcus were doing a quickie wedding sooner than expected. She put the phone to her ear, tried to let her smile be heard as she said, "Good morning, I was just thinking about calling you all."

"Why would you need to call us? I mean, we do watch the news. So anytime we need to know anything about your life, all we have to do is turn on CNN," Carmella said sarcastically.

Raven knew right away that she was in trouble. Her sweet and loving step-mother was rarely sarcastic. "I'm so sorry that I didn't call everyone yesterday, but Marcus' father ambushed us with this courthouse wedding thing the moment we left the press conference."

"How did you let this happen, Raven? Your father is so upset, he just left the house to take a walk and cool off."

"Please don't be mad at me. Senator Allen is very forceful and Marcus just wanted to stop his father from worrying."

"We're not mad at you, Raven, just disappointed. Out of all the girls, you're the one who wanted a wedding and to have 'your day' the most. Your father and I were excited about being able to make all your dreams come true on your special day."

Hearing Carmella say that made Raven think about Marcus' statement about not being able to give her a dream wedding, but being able to give her a marriage that most women only dreamed about. He was such a liar.

"If it makes you feel any better, I think I made a huge mistake. I wish I had called you and Dad and asked for your advice before just blindly following Marcus."

"What's wrong? What has happened after not even twenty-four hours of marriage?"

"He's a liar, that's what happened. And God only knows what other atrocities he's guilty of."

"He seems like a very nice man. Are you sure he lied to you?"

Her step-mother was such a good hearted person that she naturally gave everyone the benefit of the doubt and did her best to think positively. But that wasn't the way the world worked. And certainly not the political arena in which she lived, moved and did business. It was a snake pit, and Raven had to be three steps ahead of the political beings in Virginia, Maryland and D.C. or she would get a snake bite. "I'm at work now, let me call you back later."

"Wait," Carmella called out. "Let me pray for you before we get off the phone."

That put a smile on Raven's face, she could use some good old fashioned prayer right about now. "Thanks, I need all the prayer you can send my way."

As Carmella called out to God on Raven's and Marcus' behalf, it was almost as if Raven felt a shift in the atmosphere. She'd left Marcus' home, vowing never to return, but as Carmella asked God to soften Raven's heart and to bless the union of Raven and Marcus and keep them strong as they remembered to keep God first in their lives, Raven began to wonder if she had been too hasty. Her child still needed a father and if Marcus could just come clean with her, maybe they could make their marriage work.

"Amen, in Jesus name I pray," Carmella said as she finished her prayer.

"Wow, I don't know how you did it, but your prayer took away all the anger I was feeling towards Marcus."

"Prayer works, my dear," Carmella told her.

Stepping out of her car, Raven headed towards her office. "I need you to pray for me more often. Maybe I'll stop making such dumb decisions." She opened the door to her office and then said, "Oh and can you please give Daddy a big hug from me and tell him how sorry I am about everything?"

"I'll do that for you, if you'll do me a favor."

"You name it, and I'll do it."

"Pray for your husband."

***

Raven hadn't even had time to pray for herself. The minute she walked into her office, Joe was ready to go.

"I've got an idea," he told her.

"Would you mind enlightening me?" she asked as she hopped in the passenger side of Joe's Mustang.

As he drove down the street, he said, "I printed off a photo of Senator Allen and of Governor Allen, your husband..." he allowed those words to take root for a moment and then continued, "I figured we'd head back to that rehab and check with some of the nurses and patients;

maybe one of them saw something the other night that could point us in the right direction."

"That's good, but why are we showing anyone Senator Allen's picture? He doesn't have anything to do with Britney."

"While you were off getting married, I've been snooping around with some of Britney's friends. In the last few months two of her friends remembered seeing Britney in the company of the senator. And we both know how he is with the ladies, so putting it all together I discovered that after the senator's other mistress disappeared, he evidently took up with Britney."

"You're kidding?" Raven rubbed her hands across her face. "This can't be happening. My so-called father-in-law is a monster."

"You married into that family. You must like monsters," Joe said, taking his eyes off the road for a split second to look her way.

"You don't know the half of it." Raven closed her eyes as she realized the magnitude of secrets her husband was keeping from her. Mama-Carmella wanted her to pray for him, but she wanted to throttle him.

# Chapter 8

"What are you doing here?" Raven walked up on Marcus as if she wanted to swing on him.

"Same thing you're doing here... trying to find out where Britney is. Why are you so angry?"

"Because you're just trying to get in my way. But I don't care what you do, you're not going to stop me from finding Britney." She turned, getting ready to storm off, but Marcus grabbed hold of her arm and turned her back to face him. "Let me go," Raven demanded.

"I will let you go when you get it through your thick head that we are on the same team. I married you, for God's sake, what do you think I did that for?"

"Maybe you wanted to keep an eye on me so you could stop me from finding out what your father has done to another one of his lovers," she whispered, not wanting everyone in the rehab facility to hear what they were talking about.

Marcus pulled Raven to the side. "How did you find out about that?"

"Some secrets are hard to keep. You just remember that, Governor Allen."

"Oh, so I'm just the governor now. Last night I was a whole lot more, at least that's what you kept whispering in my ear."

"Don't you throw last night in my face. You tricked me into marrying you when you knew that Britney was long gone from this facility."

Joe rushed over to the couple and said, "Y'all might want to take this lover's quarrel somewhere else. We're done here anyway. Nobody remembers seeing the governor or his father."

"So, you're out here checking up on me?" Marcus shook his head as if he couldn't believe the predicament he was in.

"We just want to find Britney," Joe said.

"And if I could help, I would. But I don't know where Britney went. I have no idea why she signed herself out."

"Why don't you seem to care that Judge Hartman is worried sick about her child?" Raven asked with hands on hips, giving him plenty of attitude.

"Judge Hartman is worried about her next election. She should have worried more about Britney when she was a child. I guarantee you that Britney wouldn't be the head case that she is now, if your wonderful and honorable Judge Hartman had taken better care of Britney when she needed it the most."

Raven was silent a moment, processing the things her husband had said. He'd known the Hartmans a long time and would be privy to things she didn't know. Raven hated surprises when dealing with clients. She wanted to pick her husband's brain, but with the way she had been treating him, Raven doubted he'd be willing to tell all.

While she was trying to readjust her attitude, Joe said, "Britney's roommate said she mentioned something about a place outside the city limits. It didn't make much sense to me at first, but I think I should check it out."

"I'm going with you," Raven said.

"Oh no you're not," Marcus corrected. "My wife isn't getting ready to run around on some wild-goose chase. And anyway, I need you with me tonight."

First of all, she didn't like being told what she could and couldn't do. Secondly, who was he to think that she'd go anywhere with him? Before opening her mouth to verbalize that a still small voice reminded her, "He's your husband". She then fixed her face and said, "Joe and I are still working, why do you need me with you tonight?"

"I have to be at my father's house to discuss campaign strategy," he glanced at his watch, "in about an hour. As my wife, I feel you should be there."

And if she was there that would give her the chance to quiz his father about Britney. Raven walked Joe a few feet away from Marcus and said, "Can you go check out your lead without me? I think I might be able to get an audience with the senator if I go to this meeting. That way, before the night is over, maybe one of us will find the answers to this puzzle."

"Good deal, boss. I'll check in with you when I'm done." Joe waved at Marcus and then headed out.

As Raven got into Marcus' car, he said, "Thanks for attending this meeting with me. My step-mother will be there and whenever she starts pressuring me I end up with a splitting headache."

"What does she pressure you about?"

"You name it. If my father wants it, Liza makes it her personal business to needle me until I cave in and my father has what he wants. I don't know why it's like that, but the two of them have been tag teaming me since my mother passed."

His comment made Raven feel a little guilty, because she hadn't thought once about Marcus' needs; she'd only agreed to come to this meeting because she wanted an audience with his father. But now she could see that her role should have been bigger than that. "I've got your back, don't worry."

***

As they arrived at the senator's house, the valet took the keys from Marcus and parked the car. The two then took the expansive stairs up to the front door of his father's twenty room mansion. Marcus knocked on the door and it was immediately opened by a very stern looking gentlemen in a black suit with white gloves on.

*Seriously*, Raven thought, *who wears gloves inside the house? And who even needs a butler in this day and age... can't these people get up and answer their own door?*

Liza floated down the hall to greet them. "Come on in, you two. Your father and I have been brainstorming with your new campaign manager all afternoon."

They followed her into the library. A young, hip looking man was standing next to Marcus' father. The man extended his hand to Marcus. "I'm Brian Silverman. Your father's been getting me up to speed on everything." As he said, 'everything' he looked toward Raven as if she was the problem that needed to be managed.

"Just what has the senator been telling you?" Raven asked, not caring that her tone was far from polite.

"Excuse us for a moment," Marcus said as he guided Raven back into the hallway. "What are you doing? You don't even know this man, why are you starting the conversation with a chip on your shoulder?"

She'd witnessed her sister, Joy and her sisters-in-law acting like total loons during their pregnancies. She'd promised herself that she would never send her husband through what she had witnessed but here she was, acting just as irritable and crazy as the rest. But that didn't mean she had to admit that her hormones were raging out of control due to her pregnancy. Raven would rather throw the ball back in his court. "You don't know the man, either. How can you call yourself any kind of credible candidate for office when you let your mommy and daddy dress you up and send you out to play?"

He pointed at her, getting ready to bark back, but then he shook his head. "What's the use, just be nice, okay?"

She nodded, feeling as if she had gone too far with her comment, so keeping her mouth shut was probably the smart thing to do.

He put his hand on the doorknob getting ready to go back into the library, but then he looked back at Raven and added, "And just so you know, I've been dressing my own self and deciding when it was time to play since I was a kid. My father won't change that and neither will my wife." He swung the door back open and stepped in.

Raven grabbed hold of the door before it closed on her and followed Marcus in. She'd rarely seen Marcus angry, but she had hit a nerve. Raven realized that it was probably best to get off that nerve with the quickness, so she was all smiles and warmness as she re-entered the room.

Marcus held out a hand to her as he said, "Brian, I didn't get a chance to introduce you to my lovely wife. This is Raven. As I'm sure my father told you, we've been married for an entire day."

Brian shook Raven's hand. "It's nice to meet you, ma'am. But your reputation precedes you. I'm only surprised that we are just now meeting."

"Really?" Raven said. "Why is that?"

Explaining himself, Brian went on to say, "I've handled campaigns for two of your very satisfied clients. I've been told that your public relations firm is second to none in this city."

"Thank you for the compliment, we do our best." Feeling a little tired, Raven took a seat on the snow white sofa.

After a little more chit chat Marcus and Brian got down to business. "My step-mother tells me that you all have been discussing my campaign this afternoon."

"Only in the broadest terms," Senator Allen quickly explained. "We wanted to wait until you arrived to get down to the nuts and bolts of the matter."

The group sat down, Marcus joining Raven on the sofa. "I'd like to hear what you have in mind for this campaign. I think the biggest struggle I'm going to have is that I only have a year for the people in my state to get to know me before they decide if I'm worthy of another term."

"I agree that that could be a potential hurdle, but if we position things right, we should be able to turn that difficulty into a win for us," Brian said.

"What are your suggestions?" Raven asked.

Brian turned to her. "As a PR professional you know how important having the correct image will be for Marcus' success. So, the first thing we need to do is show his state his love for his wife and when the baby comes, we'll do a bunch of photo ops, showing how good he is with the baby."

"But what does any of that have to do with his work as a governor?" Raven asked, annoyed at the fact that she and her baby would be reduced to being nothing more than photo ops.

"We're getting to that. But I need you both to understand how important it is for the two of you to look the part of love birds. The baby will be here before we know it and we will already have whispers about you being pregnant before the marriage. So, we need to show that this is nothing other than a love connection."

Raven glanced over at Marcus wondering how he felt about acting as if he was over the moon in love with her, when she knew full well that he wasn't.

Brian continued, "No fighting in public… no distance between the two of you when you're walking into a room. Always hold hands or allow Marcus to put his arm around your shoulder."

"I love my wife, so I won't have a hard time showing that no matter where we are. But you need to know that my wife has a very spirited personality, if you haven't pinpointed that yet, so I can't guarantee the 'no arguing in public' part of your request."

Raven poked his arm with her elbow. "I'll give you spirited… I'm just fine and can handle my part. You just need to stop getting on my nerves and do what I tell you."

Pointing at his wife, Marcus said, "See what I'm talking about."

Brian laughed and then leaned back in his seat, "Actually I do... this could work."

"Okay, what else?" Marcus asked.

"We need to work on your platform," Brian said.

Liza interjected, "And while Brian thinks that family life is most important, your father and I think that your platform is the thing you need to concern yourself with most."

Marcus nudged Raven, she glanced at him, reminding herself that she didn't need to be at war with him, but his family was another matter. "Platform is very important, but I wasn't aware that Marcus had decided on one yet."

"I haven't," he told her.

"That's why I'm here," Brian said. "Your father and I think that now is the perfect time for you to have a Unity First platform."

Raven was familiar with the term. It was one recently being toss around by politicians as a way of uniting the religious right with the gay community. It was ludicrous to presume that Bible believing Christians would fall for such a scam, just because politicians put together a campaign and everything was right and good about this new world order. She sat back for a moment to see how the father of her unborn child would handle this situation.

"What exactly is this Unity First all about?" Marcus asked.

"It's basically a movement that has been gaining steam over the last few years. Christian organizations have been dropping their objection to gay marriage and even implementing inclusion practices within their policy guidelines,"

Brian said as if this was the dawn of a great new day for Christendom.

Marcus scooted up in his seat as he asked, "Are you telling me that Christian pastors are saying that gay marriage is okay even though the Bible they preach out of every Sunday says differently?"

"The movement hasn't really taken hold in most of the Christian churches yet," Brian admitted, "But they have been making headway with a lot of the Christian funded organizations."

Marcus snapped his fingers. "I just read something about this. An organization that relies heavily on donations from Christians just tried to change its policies to be inclusive of gay marriage. But I thought the backlash from that was so severe that the organization changed the policy right back."

"They did. But we believe that it's time to let the bigots of this world know that they can't stop change. Heck, if we have to we'll throw them out of our country and outlaw that outdated Bible they're always pointing to." Brian laughed along with Senator Allen and Liza at a joke that neither Raven nor Marcus seemed to get.

"So this is only a free country for the people who wish to live against the precepts of God. But the ones who want to live for God need to find another country to live in; is that what you're saying?" Raven demanded of Brian.

As Brian started stuttering, Liza walked over to Marcus and put her hand on his shoulder. "Marcus, dear, the right platform can take you all the way to the White House. Your father only wants the best for you. So, be a dear and think it over, okay?"

Marcus bent his head, put his thumbs on his temples and began massaging his forehead.

Raven leaned closer to him and asked, "What's wrong?"

"My head is killing me. I can't concentrate with my head pounding like this." He tried standing up, but plopped back into his seat as if the room had spun him around.

Raven was shaken by Marcus' condition, but his father and Liza didn't seem disturbed at all.

Liza grabbed a pill bottle out of her husband's desk drawer and began walking back towards Marcus with it. She said to Raven, "Marcus never told you about his condition. He gets these debilitating headaches from time to time. His father and I are usually left to make decisions for him… that is until he recovers."

Liza held out three small white pills to Marcus. Raven took them from her, "What are you giving him?"

"Pain medication, of course," Liza said as if Raven was being silly for even asking.

Marcus was moaning and thrashing about, Raven felt so sorry for him that she was about to hand him the pills, but then she remembered something Mama-Carmella had made her promise to do… *pray for your husband.*

Raven threw the pills on the floor and then put her hand on Marcus' head and began calling out to God as she had heard her father and Mama-Carmella do on countless occasions. "Lord Jesus, we thank You and we praise You for Your goodness. You're a wonderful God… You're a healing God and so we come to You now, asking that You look down on Marcus. Heal him as only You can. We thank You in advance for all that You do for us. Marcus needs You to show up and take away the pain that is raging through his head. In Jesus' name I pray." Raven kept her head bowed a moment while her hands lingered on Marcus' head.

"Well." Liza put her hand against her heart. "If you pray like that in public, people will think you're some kind of religious nut or something."

Marcus lifted his head with a smile on his face. He told the group, "She can be as religious as she wants to be. My headache is gone and that's all I care about."

Senator Allen stepped forward. "How'd you do that? I've had multiple tests run on him since he was a teenager. No doctor has ever been able to tell me why his headaches are so severe. But whenever one comes on him, he's usually out for hours."

*What? It worked?* was what she wanted to say, but then she remembered that the God of her parents had always been a prayer answering God. She just had never known Him to answer any of *her* prayers, since most of her prayers had consisted of requests for a husband. But wait, she now had the husband. Gleefully, Raven realized that although the Allen family had all the money and power they could handle, they didn't have the one thing that could truly make a difference in a life... they didn't have Jesus. She would never forget the lesson she'd learned tonight. "Thank You, Lord Jesus, for being a God who answers prayer."

# Chapter 9

"How did you know that prayer would work for my headache?" Marcus asked Raven as they got out of the car and headed into the house.

"I didn't. But when you started thrashing around and holding your head like that, all I could think about was the last conversation I had with my step-mother when she made me promise to pray for you."

"I knew that woman was an angel." He touched his head. "I can't believe that my headache is gone. When one of those gets started it can last all night."

"It seemed like your head didn't start hurting until your step-mother stood behind you."

"She's always around when I get one of those headaches."

"Do you have a problem with her or something? I know you said she needles you until you end up doing whatever your father wants, but she seems like a nice enough lady."

"Nice enough to you. But she and I have never gotten along. Maybe it's my fault. My dad married her so soon after my mother's death that I barely had time to grieve the passing of one mom before he was trying to shove another one in my face."

"My parents are real big on forgiveness. Maybe if you try to forgive Liza for whatever you perceive her shortcomings are, then you'll be able to be in a room with her without having a migraine."

"Or maybe, I just need to keep you with me at all times." He pulled her close to him, taking in the scent of her hair... her perfume. He was captivated by the woman in his arms. He could hold her for a lifetime and never get enough. He wanted to tell her that, but he saw the way she had looked at him when he'd told Brian that he loved his wife. She didn't believe him, so words weren't going to change her mind. He needed to show her that he was in this marriage for real.

He leaned down and put his lips to her lips. Slowly, at first, but when she didn't pull away Marcus became emboldened in his quest to show just how much love he was feeling for her. Wrapping her tighter in his arms as he moved her closer and closer towards their bedroom, he greedily clung to her mouth as if he hungered and thirsted for only her.

They were both panting and out of their minds by the time they reached the bedroom, but as they stepped into the room, a bit of sanity struck Raven and she moved away from him, clinging to the wall next to the bed. "What am I doing? I'm not supposed to be here," she said as her chest heaved in and out.

"You're my wife, Raven. Where do you belong, if not here?" The look of hurt and pain on Marcus' face was unmistakable.

"I'm sorry, Marcus, maybe we rushed into this. I never should have married you, especially since I knew what your father had in store for you."

"What are you talking about?" Marcus demanded.

Raven closed her mouth and turned away from him.

Anger poured out of Marcus as he said, "I'm your husband. Doesn't that count for anything with you? We should have no secrets."

Sighing heavily, Raven took hold of Marcus' hand and sat down next to him on the bed. "You're right. I can't keep this from you any longer because it doesn't just affect you, but me and our child as well."

Marcus was silent so she continued, "The reason I dropped your father as a client was because he wanted me to prepare you for this campaign you're getting ready to take on."

"Why wouldn't you have wanted to work with me? I mean, we were seeing each other at the time."

"I didn't have a problem with working with you," Raven tried to explain, "I had a problem with the platform your father wants you to run on... the one Brian introduced to you tonight."

"My father had this planned, even before Governor Lewis resigned?"

She nodded. "He wants you to start with this Christians-need-to-be-reasonable thing and then once you're elected President of the US of A your father's ultimate goal is to have you outlaw Christianity. How'd you like to be the president who's responsible for something like that?"

"I wouldn't like that at all," Marcus said, with a look of astonishment on his face.

Raven touched her belly. "Our child wouldn't like that either, especially since I plan to raise him or her with the same Christian values I was raised with."

"Who's stopping you?"

"Your father would love to stop me and everyone else who doesn't agree with his agenda."

Marcus paced the floor, not wanting to believe what he was hearing but at the same time knowing that it was true. He had idolized his father and had made career decisions based on conversations with his father. And now he was learning that he'd just been a pawn in his father's rule-the-world scheme.

"So now you understand why I can't stay with you. If we get a divorce now at least we can tell our child that we had been married and that the marriage just didn't work." Raven put her hand on the doorknob, getting ready to leave the bedroom.

"And then what? You're just going to leave me and tell my child how evil I was when everything my father wants comes to pass?"

"What else can I do? I have my baby to think about." Raven opened the door, put one foot on the other side.

"You can stay with me and be my prayer warrior."

Raven took her hand off the doorknob and turned back towards her husband. "How can I be your prayer warrior? I have to be reminded by my family to pray as it is."

"Well you certainly got God's attention tonight." Marcus took Raven's hands in his and pulled her closer. "If what you say is true and my father is only interested in destroying Christianity, I can't be a part of that. My mother loved the Lord and she prayed that I would follow after God all the days of my life. I haven't done much following up to this point, but that doesn't mean I want to destroy the faith my mother stood on until her dying day… help me, Raven."

Her heart went out to him and then she began to wonder if being with Marcus was what God had intended for her life's purpose all along. She thought back to the sermon that Mama-Carmella's pastor had preached out of Numbers 25 about Phinehas, the man who took a stand against the immorality of his day while others just stood around weeping and complaining about it. "I'll tell you what, Marcus, if you'll be my Phinehas then I'll stay with you."

"Who is Phinehas?" Marcus asked, his eyes clearly indicating confusion.

"Do you have a Bible?"

Marcus opened his night stand drawer and handed her the big family Bible that had been handed down from his mother. Raven turned to the book of Numbers, chapter 25 and was astonished to see the verses the pastor had read a few weeks ago highlighted in Marcus' family Bible. She pointed at the page. "The scriptures I wanted to show you are already highlighted in this Bible."

"Let me see that." The Bible was big enough for both of them to hold either side of it. As Marcus looked at the pages he said, "That's right, I remember seeing my mother highlight certain pages of the Bible as she read it. She would even call me over to her bed those last few weeks of her life and read scriptures to me." His mind shifted back into the past and he saw his mother pointing at the Bible and saying, *'Remember these words. You are a man of God and one day you will be forced to stand and declare that to the world'*.

"My mom prophesied over my life after reading from the book of Numbers. I remember wondering why God would name a book of the Bible Numbers."

Raven pointed at the Bible again. "She highlighted and underlined this." She began reading from the eleventh verse of Numbers 25:

*"Phinehas, the son of Eleazar, the son of Aaron the priest, hath turned my wrath away from the children of Israel, while he was zealous for my sake among them, that I consumed not the children of Israel in my jealousy.*

*Wherefore say, behold, I give unto him my covenant of peace: and he shall have it, and his seed after him, even the covenant of an everlasting priesthood; because he was zealous for his God, and made an atonement for the children of Israel."*

"That's me... or at least, that's what my mom expects from me." Marcus took a deep breath. "That's a lot to live up to."

Raven squeezed his hand. "We'll do it together."

\*\*\*

The next morning Marcus got out of bed and went to the kitchen to fix breakfast for Raven. They were in the early stages of being husband and wife so he wasn't sure about all the breakfast foods she liked, but he knew that she loved pancakes. So, that's what he fixed.

He didn't know whether Raven had cast a spell on him or not, but all he wanted to do was to put a smile on her face. Putting the pancakes, syrup and tall glass of ice cold milk on the tray, he headed back upstairs to the woman he married, the woman he wanted to spend the rest of his life with and have a half dozen kids if she so desired.

"Wake up sleepy head, it's time for breakfast."

Raven stretched and yawned. She then rubbed her eyes as she tried to get her bearings. "Is it morning already?"

"I must have tired you out last night, huh?" He put the tray in front of her as she sat up in bed.

"Whatever, man." Looking at the clock on the nightstand she responded, "Or maybe I just don't get up at 7 am on Saturday mornings. Don't you ever sleep in, or did I marry some kind of machine-like man?"

"Of course I sleep in." He put up a finger, halting that thought. "But never past eight. Today, however, is different. You and I have some house cleaning to do."

"Your the governor. You don't do housecleaning. You have people for that, remember?" Raven cut up her pancakes and then poured the syrup over them.

"I'm not talking about here. We need to go to your apartment and get your things."

The fork was in her hand, moving toward her mouth as she was anxious to taste his pancake. But when he mentioned getting her things and moving them in here, the fork dropped and her mouth closed.

"You're my wife, Raven. For better or worse. If our marriage is going to work, we will have to make an effort. I'm all in, what about you?"

Raven took a moment to look into the eyes of the gorgeous, successful man in front of her. He could have any woman he wanted, but he was here with her, asking her to commit to be here with him. "I'm all in."

Marshall leaned forward and kissed her. This felt good and right to him. Like coming home and loving where he lived. "Eat up. I'll go see if Beatrice can help us pack up your things."

Beatrice was one of the housekeepers and she was always willing to help or do whatever was needed to make Marcus feel at home.

Since Marcus was now living in the Governor's mansion she didn't need to bring any of her furniture. So, she and Beatrice got busy boxing up clothes and personal items. Marcus volunteered to box up her home office. While pulling files out of the draws and putting them in the boxes he'd spread out around the small room, he came across a binder that said,' *My Dreams*'.

He put the binder in the box along with the other items and tried to go back to what he was doing. But something drew him back to that binder. Marcus really didn't want to pry into Raven's life, but if his wife had dreams and aspirations, he wanted to know about them. Sitting down on the floor he opened the binder and skimmed through it.

The binder had three sections" personal, business and spiritual. The business and spiritual section had a few typed pages on her goals of growing her business and a few facts about how her spiritual life had waned and steps she intended to take in order to get back on track. It impressed him that his wife was so organized.

But when he flipped over to the personal section and noted that the only thing that seemed to matter to Raven in this section was her wedding, he realized just how badly he'd messed up by getting her to agree to simply allow a judge to marry them.

Raven didn't just have typed notes in this section. She'd glued a white wedding gown that strapless with a dipped neckline. An A-line skirt with delicate bedding all around the skirt. It was beautiful and Marcus knew instantly that the dress would be breathtaking on Raven.

The next page had two bride's maid dresses, one soft pink and the other rose. There were pages and pages of dried flowers lamented to a page. She'd even taken pictures of table settings at wedding receptions and a three-tiered cake with snowy white frosting had the words, 'this is my cake' written next to it. "What have I done?" Marcus scolded himself as he closed the binder and put it back in the box.

"I hope you haven't messed up my file system," Raven said as she walked in the room all smiles.

Jumping up, Marcus put another pile of folders over the binder. "You think I don't know how to handle a filing system. Woman, I'll have you know, you're not the only one in this family with organizational skills."

She nodded. "Okay, your right, I have seen your office. And you do seem to know what you're doing."

"That's high praise coming from you." He bent down and touched her lips to his for a quick kiss. He enjoyed kissing his wife and planned to do as much of it as she'd let him get away with.

"I was getting ready to order some lunch. Is pizza okay with you?"

"Sounds good. Get mine with pepperonis and sausage."

"Got it."

As she walked out of the room, Marcus wanted to grab her, pull her into his arms and tell her just how sorry he was that she didn't get the wedding of her dreams. But he had just convinced her to give being married to him a try, so he didn't want to throw salt in a fresh wound.

They went to Marcus' family church on Sunday. His parent's sat next to them and no sooner than service was over did they start badgering him about his next meeting with the campaign manager they hand picked her him.

Marcus stepped back and lifted a hand to get their attention. "Look, I appreciate your help, Dad. You know I do. But you and I seem to have a difference of opinion on how my next campaign should be run."

"Since when do you and your father have a difference of opinion?" Liza snapped while glaring at Raven.

"I don't want to argue with the two of you," Marcus said quickly, hoping to avoid another headache. "I will meet with Brian tomorrow and if he can get with the kind of campaign I want to run then he may be of use to me. But if not…"

Senator Allen put a hand on his son's shoulder as he said, "I've put a great deal of money into your campaigns these last few year. I would hate to think that I've wasted my money, time and effort."

"You haven't wasted anything on Marcus," Raven declared. "He is the most dedicated man I know. He wants to win this next election just as much as you want him to win. The two of you just have different vision, that's all."

"This is none of your business," Liza told Raven. Then she turned to her husband and spat, "I told you not to hire her in the first place. Now look what you've done. We're stuck with her and Marcus' campaign is about to go down the drain."

"Thanks for that vote of confidence, Mommy Dearest."

With fire in her eyes, she screamed at Marcus, "I told you not to call me that!" Rolling her eyes, Liza slung her purse back over her shoulder and strutted away from the group.

"Why'd you have to antagonize your mother, son?"

"She's not my mother. She's your wife and that's it and all. Please stop trying to make this more than it really is," Marcus told his father.

Shaking his head, Senator Allen walked away from them and joined his wife.

"That went well." Marcus grimaced as he watched his father drive off.

Raven put her hand in his. As they strolled to Marcus' car, she told him, "I think we need to find another church to attend."

# Chapter 10

After that scene with Marcus' parent, Raven knew that if her husband was going to do the right thing, he would need back-up so she called her youngest brother, RaShawn. He had left the mission field and was now doing his mission work right here in the United States. And Raven had a mission for him.

"Are you sure Marcus will want me as part of his team?" RaShawn asked.

"Marcus isn't just my husband, he's now my client. So, if I say he needs a spiritual advisor on his team, then that's what he's going to get."

"Okay, big sis. If you say so. Just tell me when you want me to be there."

"Check your email, I've already sent you an airline ticket. Your plane leaves in two hours. I'll pick you up."

RaShawn laughed. "What if I had said no?"

"Who are you kidding, you've never been able to deny me or Renee anything."

"I guess you're right about that. Let me hang up so I can throw some clothes in my duffel. I'll see you soon."

"Thanks, RaShawn, I knew there was a reason why I love you so much." They hung up the phone, then Raven stood up and straightened her suit. "Time to go put out another fire."

She walked down the hall to Marcus' office. He was in a meeting with Brian, and had told her he would wait until she got there before giving him the ax.

As she opened the door Brian was saying, "You only have a month before you need to declare your candidacy for the next election, we really need to firm up your platform."

"Correct." Marcus stood up, came around to the front of his desk and leaned against it as he said, "I'm looking for more of a 'bring our family values back' and a 'jobs first' platform."

"But Governor, the job situation has already been improving and 'family values' has really been overdone."

Raven sat down in the back of the room, silently praying that God would continue to give her husband the strength he would need to stand strong in his convictions.

"Actually Brian, I don't think it's been done enough. This country has lost sight of its values. Look at all the filth they call entertainment that fills our televisions. I don't want my children thinking that the way these reality TV stars live is the right way to go with their lives. I'm drawing a line in the sand. We should have never allowed things to get this far, but I guarantee that I will not do anything while I'm in public office to make it worse."

Brian was practically sputtering as he stood. "Your father assured me that you were onboard with this Unity First campaign that I've started putting together for you."

Praying harder than she'd ever prayed in her entire life, Raven was still silently calling on the name of Jesus, asking the angels to come down and protect Marcus' mind, body and soul and just generally begging God to help them, not now, but right now.

"Your Unity First campaign isn't going to work for me. I don't believe that Christians need to let go of the convictions they have that are based on God's word just because another group of people want to live contrary to the word of God."

"That Bible you keep talking about is outdated. And hypocritical."

"Excuse me?" Marcus said, staring down on Brian as if he was two seconds from throwing him out of his office.

"Are you going to tell me that," he swung his arm backward, pointing in her direction, "Raven would be okay with you deciding to marry about two, three or more other women while you're still married to her?"

"Of course she wouldn't be okay with that."

"Several men in that Bible you're so proud of did exactly that. Solomon was the worst offender of them all. But your God didn't frown on that, but then he turned His righteous nose up at gay marriage… it just doesn't seem right to me."

*Keep your mouth shut and just pray*, Raven reminded herself. *Jesus, Jesus, Jesus… calling on His name all the day long.*

Marcus grinned and then said, "I'll tell you what... when I get to heaven I'll ask God about that. But will I be able to find you to give you the answer?"

Again, Brian was flustered to the point of stammering. "T-this conversation is totally pointless. We need to be working on your platform. Are you willing to go with the platform your father has already designed for your campaign or do I need to report back to the senator about this?"

Marcus sat back down behind his desk. He looked over at Brian and shook his head. "If you're not willing to readjust to the platform I want to run on, then I don't think we have anything else to talk about at this point in time. But do give my father my regards."

"Are you serious?" Brian was flabbergasted. "Do you know how many politicians would love to have my group on their team? I back winners, in case you haven't noticed. I've only taken on one client in the past twenty years who didn't win. And if I had him as a client in this day and age, he would win by a landslide."

Raven walked over to Marcus' desk as she said, "We're very happy for you, Brian. You've had an impressive career. Any candidate would be lucky to have you. However, the governor wants to go in a different direction. I'm in the process of finding your replacement as we speak."

Brian turned away from them and stormed out of the office in a huff.

"Did you really just fire him without a replacement already picked out?" Marcus put his hands on his head and shook it. He then looked back toward his wife and said, "Tell me that I've got this wrong?"

"Didn't you hire me to put your campaign team together?" Raven answered a question with a question.

"Yes, but…"

"But nothing. You need to trust me. I know what I'm doing." She waited for him to say something else; when he didn't she asked, "Do you have time in your schedule tomorrow afternoon?"

He opened his desk calendar. "What for?"

"I'd like to have you meet a few potential staffers for your campaign team."

"You're telling me that you can pull all the people that I'll need for my campaign together that quick?"

"Honey, I'm not just good at my job… I'm the best." Raven walked out of the office, leaving Marcus staring with awestruck eyes.

Stepping into the hallway, she punched a number in her cell phone. When her assistant, Rebecca answered she said, "Go through our rolodex; pull together as many Christian conservative campaign managers as you can find." As she ended the call and headed out of the building, Raven was confident that she would be able to locate the perfect person to handle Marcus' campaign. Her client didn't need to know that she just now started looking for his campaign manager.

Her cell rang when she got in her car. It was Joe. She hadn't talked to him since he left on a hunt for Britney. "Hey Joe, it is so good to hear from you. We have a new client, so, I sure hope that you have located Britney so we can put that issue to bed."

"I got her, Raven. And you will not believe what I'm witnessing right now."

"I hope it's some good news because we can really use some of that."

"Oh my God, no… don't shoot!" Joe screamed.

"Who's there, Joe? What's going on?" Raven asked as she clutched the phone tighter against her ear.

And then she heard three consecutive shots. *Bang… bang… bang.*

"Joe, Joe, what's going on?" Raven was yelling into her cell phone, then the phone went dead and she screamed as she pulled the phone away from her ear to stare at it. Had she really heard shots?

She called Joe's cell back. It rang several times and then went to voicemail. "Call me back, Joe. Right away… please."

She hung up the phone and waited a few minutes, willing her cell to ring and for Joe to be on the other end, saying that her ears deceived her and that everything was all right. She had sent Joe looking for Britney and because she was too busy with Marcus, Joe had gone alone. Raven didn't know if she could live with herself if anything happened to her friend and business associate.

When the phone didn't ring. She called Joe again and this time it rang once and then went to voicemail. "I really need you to call me. Come on, Joe, don't leave me hanging like this."

# Chapter 11

Raven went to the police station, trying to get help for Joe. But since she hadn't been able to get a location and the fact that his phone had been turned off, the police weren't able to track his whereabouts and were therefore limited in how they could help.

She left the police station disheartened, but as an idea struck, she pulled over to the side of the road and pulled out her cell phone. With the high-profile clientele they dealt with, Joe was always worried that someone might feel as if Raven knew too much and desire to get rid of her. So, he'd installed listening devices and cameras in her home, GPS tracking on her phone and car. Raven had also made sure that Joe did the same for himself in case she ever needed to track him.

Raven pushed the tracker app on her phone and hit the button to locate Joe's car. Her mouth fell open when, after searching for a few seconds, the locator pinpointed Joe's car and began giving her voice activated directions to get to it. All Raven could do was thank God for technology as she drove full speed ahead.

It took twenty minutes of following the directions from her cell phone to reach the location where Joe's BMW was parked. She pulled up behind it and was about to get out of her car when her cell phone rang.

She wouldn't have picked it up except that it was RaShawn, who she figured was at the airport and would be expecting her to pick him up in a few hours. He needed to know what she was doing in case she didn't make it to pick him up.

"Hey RaShawn, are you at the airport?"

"Yeah, my plane leaves in ten minutes. I just wanted to let you know that I should be there in about an hour."

"I need you to be praying while you're on that plane. I'm out looking for one of my business associates. I'm afraid something terrible has happened to him."

"Where are you?"

"I'm on a residential street." She looked out her window at several houses, trying to decide which address to give her brother. She said a quick prayer, asking the Lord to show her which house to go into and then she gave RaShawn the address. "Write it down," she told him. "If I'm not there to pick you up in an hour, call Marcus and have him get someone over here right away."

"Okay sis, but before you hang up, I want to pray for you."

Not knowing whether Joe was dead or alive, Raven knew she needed a lot of prayer. So she kept her seat and allowed RaShawn to pray God's protection over her life and the life of her unborn child. When he was finished praying, RaShawn said, "The Lord revealed to me that this is a spiritual battle you're in right now. You can't fight this with your own strength. Let the Lord fight this battle."

That sounded so good, but Raven wasn't sure what to do besides pray, so she asked, "How do I do that?"

"I'll be praying that God opens your eyes so that you can see that God has got this for you. You don't have to fight in your own strength because the Lord will fight this battle." An announcement was made over the loudspeaker. Then RaShawn said, "Oh God, if only I had a little more time." RaShawn sounded rushed as he said, I've got to go, sis, they're boarding my plane."

"Wait! I don't understand how the Lord fights my battles."

"Don't go in that house before reading 2 Kings, chapter six. Just start at verse fifteen. I love you, sis, I'll see you in a little bit. I'll be praying." He hung up.

Raven was left to stare at her phone. She was confused by her conversation with RaShawn. Driving over there, all she could think to do was go in this house, get Joe and get him to a hospital, if need be. She had no clue about any type of spiritual battle. Fear was gripping her heart, so she did as her brother suggested and opened the Bible app on her phone and started reading in 2 Kings:

*And when the servant of the man of God arose early and went out, there was an army, surrounding the city with horses and chariots. And his servant said to him, "Alas, my master! What shall we do?*

*So he answered, "Do not fear, for those who are with us are more than those who are with them." And Elisha prayed, and said, "Lord, I pray, open his eyes that he may see." Then the Lord opened the eyes of the young man, and he saw. And behold, the mountain was full of horses and chariots of fire all around Elisha. So when the Syrians came down to him, Elisha prayed to the Lord, and said, "Strike this people, I pray, with blindness." And He struck them with blindness according to the word of Elisha.*

So Elisha was able to make a request of the Lord to fight the battle for him and the Lord did just that. That sounded good to Raven. She was just about to put away her phone and then knock on each door until she located Joe when she received a text message that read, *What are you waiting for? Come on in.* Raven recognized the number from the text message. Senator Allen had left her text messages from this phone on two separate occasions and now he was taunting her to come inside the place where he'd taken Britney and done God knows what to Joe.

Raven had given RaShawn a street address, but she hadn't been positive that Joe was inside that house, until the door opened and no one stepped out. She texted Marcus and gave him the address to the house she was about to go into and then told him, "Call the police, your father is holding Britney hostage in this house."

Getting out of her car, Raven touched her belly as she mumbled to her baby, "Your grandfather needs Jesus in a big way."

She took a deep breath, looked towards heaven and then entered the house. "Senator, are you in here?"

\*\*\*

Marcus had plans of doing good and looking out for the people he was charged with serving, rather than trying to line his pockets or gain political points. He just hoped his constituents understood his heart even though he wasn't willing to have some gimmicky jump-on-the-bandwagon type of campaign.

But even with his political future up in the air, Marcus felt better than he had in a long, long time. He was married to a beautiful woman, they had a baby on the way and he'd just discovered that God had a purpose for his life. Nothing could be sweeter than that.

"I know that Governor Lewis was making preparations to relocate some of the governmental offices in my city to the state capital, but I'm hoping that you will reconsider this move," Mayor Taylor said.

"I reviewed the information. It seems like a sound plan. Most of the functions are already handled here in Richmond so it just makes sense to move all of them here."

"I do not agree. As governor, you should be looking out for what's best for the entire state and not just the city your offices are located in." Mayor Taylor leaned forward as he continued, "Look, Governor Allen, you have the right to do whatever you want, but I'm just asking that you consider how moving almost a thousand jobs out of my city will devastate the community that I represent."

Nodding, Marcus said, "I can appreciate how keeping those jobs in your community benefits your city. So, I'll give the plans another viewing to see if there is any way that we can keep some of the jobs in your city." Standing, Marcus put out a hand to Mayor Taylor.

Taylor rose from his seat and shook Marcus' hand. "I thank you for hearing me out. You're a good man, Marcus; if there is ever anything I can do for you, just let me know."

"I'll hold you to that come election time." Marcus grinned as if he was joking, but he was serious. Calling in favors was what politicians did for breakfast, lunch and dinner... and at birthday parties and on Christmas, too, if need be.

Marcus walked the mayor to the lobby and was headed back to his office when someone put a hand on his shoulder and turned him around. He smiled as he came face to face with his father. "Hey, what brings you to our great state this morning? No votes in the senate today?"

"I'm all voted out this week. Not that any of our votes are going to do a bit of good once they go to The House. Those clowns act like they never watched that cartoon about how a bill becomes law when they were kids." He shook his head. "I needed to get away. Thought I'd come spend some time with my son, the governor."

"I have tons of meetings today. But if you don't mind tagging along, I don't think anyone will mind. After all, you are one of the greatest senators Virginia has ever had."

"That's what they tell me." Senator Allen's smile widened as his chest puffed out.

Father and son stepped into Marcus' office. He had left his cell phone on the desk. Tapping it, Marcus leaned over the desk so he could see if he'd missed any calls. No calls, but he had a text message from Raven that caused him to snatch up the phone and then look at his father with questioning eyes.

"What's wrong?" Senator Allen asked.

"Why does my wife want me to call the police on you? Evidently she has found Britney and says that you are holding her hostage."

"I'm right here in front of you, son, so I couldn't be holding Britney hostage. And why would I want to do that anyway?"

"We both know the answer to that, don't we?"

Senator Allen grimaced. "Why do you believe Britney over your own father? I never touched that girl."

With arms folded across his chest, Marcus shook his head. "She loved you, Dad. And as confused as her mind was, she actually believed that you loved her, too."

"You just said it yourself, Marcus. Britney is a confused young woman. Don't you think it's possible that she mistook my kindness and dreamed up this whole relationship business? I'm a happily married man; why would I cheat?"

"I don't have time for this. You're here, so at least I know you're not somewhere attacking my wife."

"Of course not. I would never attack Raven."

His assistant buzzed in and informed him that his next appointment had arrived early. Marcus was about to asked that he be sent in, but something about Raven's text bothered him. Yes, his father was right in front of him. But Raven didn't just make things up. So, something was going on. "I need you to cancel the rest of my morning appointments. I have to leave the office for a little while."

"I'll get on it right now," his assistant said.

Marcus hung up the phone and grabbed his keys.

"Where are you going?" Senator Allen asked with a look of incredulity on his face.

"To see about my wife."

"You've got work to do here. I was expecting Brian to stop by again today so the three of us could go to lunch and talk over your campaign."

"Give it up, Dad. I'm not your errand boy. I'll run for office on the platform I choose, not on any of this craziness that you've involved yourself with lately... things that I don't even believe."

Senator Allen grabbed hold of his son's shoulder and pulled him toward himself. "Don't you see why I didn't want you to marry that girl? She likes to spout off about her family's Christian principles but the first chance she got she was in bed with you. Doesn't that show you that they're all just a bunch of hypocrites?"

Marcus pried his father's fingers away from his shoulder as he said, "No, it tells me that she and I made a mistake in how we handled our relationship. But thanks to you, we rectified that in a hurry. Now she's my wife and there isn't a thing in the world I wouldn't do for her... and that includes calling the police on you, if you've done something to her. Now, I have to go."

"I'm coming with you."

They rushed out of the Capitol and headed down the streets of Richmond. All that was on Marcus' mind was finding his wife and getting her out of whatever kind of trouble she had found her way into. "Lord God, we sure do need you now," was all he kept saying as he neared the location where his father was supposedly holding Britney.

# Chapter 12

Raven went from room to room looking for Britney and Senator Allen. It was a ranch style house with a basement. No one was on the main floor so Raven turned on the lights for the basement and made her way down the steps. "Senator Allen, are you down here?"

No answer.

As she touched the last step she called out, "Joe, are you here?" Rounding the corner the foul odor hit her first, then Raven's mouth flew open at the shock and horror of what she was witnessing. Three huge cages lined the unfinished walls of the basement. The one at the farthest end of the basement was empty, but the other two…

"Oh my God, Britney!" Raven exclaimed as she ran over to the second cage. "Why would he put you in this thing?"

Britney crawled to the front of the cage. She grabbed hold of the cage and pleaded, "Get out of here or you'll be next."

"I can't just leave you here. What the senator has done to you is inhumane. And I promised your mother that I would bring you home safe and I plan to do just that."

As sadness crept into Britney's eyes, she said, "My mother doesn't want me back."

"Of course she does. Why do you think we came looking for you?" Raven glanced down and noticed that there was a lock on the cage. A cot and blanket were on the floor with a bucket that must have been put there for human waste. She couldn't see what was in the bucket, but she smelled it... boy, did she smell it. "Let me find something to break that lock."

"You won't find anything. I've been looking for months," a woman in the third cage said.

Glancing over to that cage, she saw the extended belly on the woman first, then as her eyes lifted, Raven looked into the face of the woman who had made the news for more than a week after her disappearance. "Rita?"

The woman nodded. "It's me," she said as tears drifted down her face. "I've been locked in this cage for so long I don't even know what month we're in right now." Her hands held onto her belly. "But I think my baby is about to come and I'm terrified to have it delivered by the monster that's been keeping us down here."

The senator's ex-lover wasn't dead after all. He had held her in dungeon-like conditions with Britney for God knows how long. The man was truly, as Rita had proclaimed, a monster. "You won't have to deliver your baby in here. I'll get you out. I'll get both of you out."

"Just leave," Britney yelled at her. "Go outside and call the police. Or do you want to get shot like that man over there?"

"Are you talking about Joe?" Raven asked, suddenly remembering that she had come to this God forsaken place to find her friend and business associate.

Britney pointed towards the third cage. Raven rushed over to it, not knowing how she had missed the fact that a body was lying on the floor just a few feet from where she stood. She'd seen Britney and Rita, but hadn't noticed that anyone was in the third cage... probably because he was on the opposite side of the mattress and in the fetal position. "Joe, oh my Lord, Joe, please say something to me," she said as she stepped into the open, unlocked cage and frantically checked for a pulse.

It was faint, but there was a pulse. "Don't you die on me. I'm going to go get help and get you out of here. But you've got to wait for me, okay, Joe?" Tears were in her eyes as she tried to convince herself that she would be able to get help and get back to them in enough time to keep Joe alive.

"I'll be back for all of you." She stood up, preparing to leave when the door to the cage was slammed shut.

"You're not going anywhere."

Raven heard the words, and by the time she swung around to see what was going on, the lock had been snapped on the cage and a gun was being pointed in her face.

Britney had tried to warn her. She should have never entered the house without calling the police first, but she had been so worried about Joe that she hadn't been thinking. She was thinking now, though, and wondering how she was ever going to get out of this messy situation. She wasn't just worried about Joe living. With the lock on the cage and that gun in her face, Raven wondered if she would live to give birth to the child she was carrying.

\*\*\*

The moment RaShawn got off the plane, he texted his sister, **Are you okay?**

By the time he picked up his bags she still hadn't responded. As fear for his sister tried to clench his heart, RaShawn carefully reminded himself of who he was and who he belonged to. And he knew with everything in him that the God he served would never let him down.

Raven had asked him to call Marcus for a ride if she didn't arrive by the time he got off the plane, but RaShawn didn't feel like hanging around the airport waiting when he needed to get to his sister. He got into a taxi and gave the man the address Raven had given him. Once the taxi was on its way, RaShawn placed a call to Marcus. When Marcus answered he told him everything Raven had said to him before he got on the plane.

"She sent me a text. I'm on my way to that house right now."

"Good, then I'll meet you there," RaShawn told him.

"My father is with me so hopefully we can get to the bottom of whatever is going on. I just don't want anything to happen to Raven."

"Then we need to pray."

"I'll be praying," Marcus said, "but, RaShawn, I need you to pray real hard, too, because I can't lose her... she means too much to me."

"Ditto," RaShawn replied as they hung up.

\*\*\*

"Put the gun down. You don't have to do this," Raven said as she backed away from the cage door, hands in the air.

"You shouldn't have meddled in our business. And you shouldn't have gotten yourself knocked up by Marcus. You're nothing but a tramp, looking for a meal ticket."

Raven wouldn't have believed it if she wasn't seeing this with her own eyes, but Liza Allen, the senator's wife, was holding a gun on her and saying disparaging things to her about being pregnant by Marcus. She understood why Liza would be upset about Rita being pregnant by the senator, but what she and Marcus did was between them and God. "Why are you upset about my baby? I would think you and the senator would be happy for a grandchild."

Liza laughed bitterly at that. "You, and these tramps," she pointed towards the other cages, "think you can flaunt your babies in front of me and I'm just supposed to sit there and take it like I'm some joke. Well, the joke is on you... on all of you."

"What are you talking about Liza? I don't understand. Just let us go. I need to get Joe to the hospital."

"He's as good as dead. And none of you are going anywhere until you deliver those unwanted babies."

Raven knew that she was pregnant and Rita was, but was Liza saying that Britney was also pregnant? Raven glanced in Britney's direction and the confirmation was all over her face.

Smiling, Britney said, "It was the best thing that ever happened to me. I even decided to get clean. And then this psycho took me out of rehab with her lies."

"I'd rather be a liar than a slutty home wrecker," Liza shot back. She then turned back to Raven with her hand extended. "Give me your cell phone and car keys."

"What?" Raven shook her head, she needed that cell phone. And she would need her keys the moment she found a way out of this cage.

Liza pointed the gun at her belly. "Give them to me or I'll put a bullet right through your baby's heart."

All the fight went out of Raven. She handed over her keys and the cell phone.

When Raven gave up her cell phone, Rita became panic stricken. Her hands gripped the bars of her cage as she shook it. "I'm so sorry that I slept with your husband. If I could take it all back I would in a heartbeat. But please, Liza, please don't harm my baby because of what I did."

Liza stormed over to Rita's cage with fire in her eyes. "Don't you talk to me about doing no harm. When I called and begged you not to do that interview about your torrid affair with my husband, what did you do? You laughed in my face and told me that you didn't care what happened to me or the senator. Well, now I'm returning the favor, because I don't care what happens to you or that unwanted baby."

From dealing with Liza on different occasions, Raven knew that the senator's career and legacy were all that mattered to her. So, she played on that now, hoping that the woman would come to her senses and release them from their cages. "What you're doing isn't right, Liza. The senator's career will never recover from this. You need to let all of us go now and then issue a public apology."

"I don't need you to fix any situation for me, Raven." Liza then pointed at Joe and said, "Just shut up and play with your little pet."

***

RaShawn hated getting his parents involved, because he really didn't want to worry them. But his spirit man was tugging on him, telling him that Raven had gotten involved in some serious spiritual warfare and if he was going to get her out of it, he needed everybody praying.

When his dad answered the phone, RaShawn hurriedly asked, "What are you all doing?"

"Oh, just sitting around the table with Carmella, Ronny and Nia working on the final plans for this upcoming wedding."

"I'm glad that Ronny is there with you all because I need to tell you something."

"What's up, son? How was your flight? Is everything okay?"

"No Dad, it's not. Raven is missing. I'm on my way to where I think she might be, but the Lord has revealed to me that she is involved in something that man can't get her out of… not in our own strength, anyway. So, I need you all to stop what you're doing and go to war through prayer and praise until I call you back."

Ramsey's voice was shaky as he said, "You got it, son. Just go get Raven and bring her out of whatever this is safely."

They hung up the phone without saying another word. RaShawn wished he could tell his father that everything was going to be all right, but in truth, he just didn't know. "Open Raven's eyes, Lord, help her to see what she is up against and then lead her and guide her in the way to get out."

# Chapter 13

"Oh God, oh God, please don't let him die." Raven was bent down on the ground next to Joe, pressing the wound trying to stop the blood from continuing to flow out of him. "You are such a good man, Joe. Don't give up. Don't let her win."

As far as Raven was concerned Liza was crazy. The woman had left reality and was living in some weird world where she thought she could... what? Stop babies from being delivered? It was all too crazy and bizarre for Raven to figure out. She'd thought that Rita had been killed by the senator in order to shut her up. In her wildest imagination, she never would have imagined that anyone would hold human beings hostage for months.

But hadn't that sick man in Cleveland, OH held those three women and a baby for ten years before his secret was discovered? And what about that Jaycee Lee Dugard case? The woman had been held for eighteen years and even had a couple of kids while in captivity. Thinking of those cases brought tears to her eyes. She didn't want Joe to die on the floor and she didn't want to spend years in this basement. She had a life, a family and a husband and she desperately wanted to see them all again.

As her tears were dripping all over Joe, Raven realized that she wasn't helping him much by just crying. So, she closed her eyes and started praying. As she was pouring out her heart to God she finally remembered the scriptures that RaShawn had asked her to read before coming into this house of horrors. Elisha had prayed and God had fought his battle. Through her sobs, Raven prayed, "Lord, I don't know what's going on here. But *You* know, and I'm asking that You take care of this for me. I need You and as many angels as You can spare to fight this battle for me."

After that prayer, it felt to Raven as if her eyelids were suddenly pulled open and the room was filled with smoke. Coughing, she yelled out, "Where'd all of this smoke come from? Is she trying to set us on fire?"

"I don't see any smoke," Britney said. "The wicked witch went upstairs, but I didn't see her light anything before she went."

Still coughing, Raven kept one hand on Joe's stomach and tried to fan the thick clouds of smoke in front of her with the other. "Lord, help us; get this smoke out of here."

As the smoke began to clear, Raven wanted to pray it back. Anything would have been better than what she was now witnessing. Monster-like creatures were standing guard in front of their cages. One of them glared into her cage with nostrils flaring. His big paw-like hands rattled the cage as he screamed, "Stop praying!"

"Never!" Raven screamed back and started calling down angels to help her. Thank God RaShawn asked her to read that scripture concerning Elisha, when the enemies of the Lord came against him. But Elisha didn't waiver because he knew that those that were with him were more than those that were with his enemy. "You can't win this fight. God is greater and He'll never let you win."

The creature didn't look as hateful as he stood there and laughed at her. Then his eyes turned cold as they bore into her. "We've already won. You Bible thumpers are just too stupid to know when you've been beaten."

"We're not stupid. We see that you've infiltrated the world and filled it with sin. But my Bible tells me that where sin abounds, grace does much more abound. So, you keep pulling people into sin, and I and people like my brother and my husband will pull them right back out. God will win this battle."

"Who is she talking to?" Britney asked Rita.

"I don't know, but she's hasn't been in that cage a full hour yet, so there's no way she could have lost her mind that quick."

"I haven't lost my mind," Raven told them. "But if you two want to get out of here alive I suggest you get on your knees and start praying. Ask the Lord to forgive you of your sins and pray that He would unlock the chains that bind us." Raven was doing the same; the only difference was that her eyes were open to the demonic forces around them. She could see clearly that those demons were not going to let them just pray their way out of this. They were gearing up for a fight. Raven only prayed that God's avenging angels would get there in time enough to give them the last fight of their ungodly lives.

***

"There it is," Marcus said after his GPS told him that he had arrived at his destination. He pointed to the house in front of them.

Senator Allen turned to his son with disbelief in his eyes. "This is the house Raven thought I was holding Britney in?"

"Yeah, do you recognize it?"

"Liz's mom lived here before we put her in the nursing home. I told Liz to sell the home, but she had some sort of sentimental attachment to it."

Looking around, Marcus said, "I don't see Raven's car."

"Maybe she's not here."

Something in Marcus' gut told him that wasn't the case. His wife was in that house and he had to get her out of there. "Dad, I promise you, if Liz has harmed my wife in any way, I will make her pay."

"Calm down, son. I'm sure Raven was just overreacting… pregnancy hormones kicking in or something."

"You better hope so." Marcus was scared out of his wits. His heart was beating so fast he thought it would come out of his chest. His wife and baby were in danger, and although they had only been married a short time and had only gotten married because of the pregnancy, Marcus knew that he wouldn't be able to live with himself if something happened to either of them.

The front door was locked, but Senator Allen had a key. He fumbled around, trying to remember which key unlocked the door to the small house. He got it on his third try. Opening the door, the senator yelled, "Liza, are you in here?"

\*\*\*

Liza had driven Raven's car two blocks away from the house and left it parked in a shopping center. She then got out of the car and made the trek back to her mother's old house. The place had always felt like a dungeon to Liza, especially as she grew up, trapped there with her hateful mother. Liza had never been able to please that woman; no matter what she did, her mother always had a ready complaint.

At the age of seven her mother purchased a cage, put it in the basement and told Liza that bad girls had to sleep in the cage. She had been bad a lot, but by the time she was fifteen she'd learned how to accommodate her mother and she never had to sleep in the cage again. But her mother had kept that cage all those years just to remind Liza of what bad girls had to endure.

Liza fixed her. Just as soon as she could, she had that crazy old lady placed in the worst nursing home she could find. Now she was seeing what mean old ladies had to endure.

Her husband had asked her to put the house up for sale, but for some reason, Liza hadn't been able to bring herself to do it. She knew that she would never live there ever again life, but something inside kept telling her that she would soon have a purpose for that house. And then Rita decided that having an affair with her husband wasn't good enough. She had to get pregnant and then tell the world about it. Reminding the world the Liza Allen had never been able to conceive any children of her own and that's when Liza knew what she would do with that house.

The cage was still in the basement. She met Rita for drinks, slipped her a mickey and then put her in the car and drove her to her final destination. After that, finding out about Britney and Raven, Liza purchased two more cages. She hadn't planned to put Raven in a cage at first, but the night she prayed for Marcus and took his headache away sealed her fate.

As she stepped onto her porch and noticed that the front door was ajar, Liz pulled the gun out of her purse and quietly pushed opened the front door.

***

"I hear voices below us, Dad. Does this house have a crawl space or a basement?"

"I believe it has a basement, but I've never been in it," the senator answered.

"There, did you hear that?" Marcus thought he heard faint sounds of crying and praying at the same time. He pointed downward. "There must be a basement."

They went into the kitchen, located the basement door, found a lock on it. But Marcus kept hearing those voices so he wasn't about to let a little thing like a lock stop him from getting in that basement, not when his wife was most likely down there. He stepped back and kicked the door with everything he had. As his foot touched down on the ground his knee buckled, but the basement door swung open.

Looking back at his father, he asked, "Coming?" But Marcus didn't wait for an answer. His knee was aching but he didn't care, he barreled down those stairs like a line-backer, calling out, "Raven! Raven, are you down here?"

***

They had been praying for a little under an hour when Carmella popped up and said, "This isn't getting it." She went to her stereo system, turned it on and let Hezekiah Walker's *Every Praise* drown out any and all doubt that the victory was theirs in this situation. God was their savior, He was a healer and He was a deliverer, too. Just as He had delivered all of her children out of dangerous situations, He would also deliver Raven.

"All right, let's get back to it. We are going to pray and praise God until we get the word that Raven is safe. And then we are going to go get that child and drag her back home, her husband, too, if it has to go down like that."

They all knew that Carmella was serious so no one bothered to remind her that Marcus was busy running the Common Wealth of Virginia. They just all bowed their heads again and continued praying to the only One they knew to turn to in times like these.

*\*\*\**

"Did you hear that?" Rita asked. "I think someone just kicked the door in. Raven, you're a genius, this prayer stuff really works."

Although Rita was excited, Raven wasn't jumping for joy just yet, because she could see the demonic forces that were guarding their cages. If it wasn't Jesus Himself who just kicked down that door, then they were still in trouble.

Then she heard her name and knew that her husband had come to rescue her. Immediately, she felt fear for him as two burly demons left her cage and went in search of Marcus. "Leave him alone."

"Shut up," one of the demons hissed back.

"Jesus," Raven yelled out. "I need You to send help *now*. Please don't let those monsters destroy my husband."

As she called out to God, the smoky clouds in the basement began lifting as light began shining through. The next thing she saw brought both shock and awe. Angelic beings descended, with swords drawn. They took on those menacing demons that had been guarding their cages and began dispatching them one by one back to the devil they came from.

"Thank you, Jesus, they are here!" Raven exclaimed. She lifted her hand off of Joe as she noticed an angel bend down next to her and put his hand over Joe's stomach. "Oh, thank God."

"I'm here, honey. Don't worry, I'm going to get you out of this cage."

Raven got off the floor and rushed to the front of the cage. "I knew you wouldn't leave me here. I knew you'd get my message."

"I almost didn't come. Dad was in my office when I received your text and I thought you were just falsely accusing him again." Marcus closed his eyes as a pain shot through his heart. "I could have lost you. I will never doubt you ever again." They clung to each other through the opening in the cage.

"But I was wrong about your dad. It's Liza. She's crazy, Marcus. She's been holding Rita and Britney."

"I can't believe this." Marcus' eyes widened as he turned to see who was in the other two cages. Then he said, "Let me find something to get you out of here."

"Step away from that cage, Marcus. Don't make me hurt you," Liza said as she entered the basement, gun drawn on Marcus.

Senator Allen was standing in the middle of the basement, looking as if he'd been hit with a stun gun. He had no words for what he was witnessing, but as his wife came down the stairs, pointing a gun at his son, he turned to her. "Liza, what are you doing?"

"Don't you question me," she screamed at him. "If you had been able to keep your pants up I wouldn't have to clean up your messes. But I'm the dutiful wife, so I always clean up your messes."

"I never asked you to do this. We could have weathered this storm. I only asked you to stick by my side."

She was shaking with rage now. "Oh yeah, you wanted me to endure more press conferences where I stood there holding your hand, smiling up at you like you were the great love of my life, when I knew that you had never forgiven me for not being Shavona. Well, guess what, Michael," she pointed at the cages. "These tramps aren't Shavona either. No one will ever be as self-righteous as she was, ever again. I made sure of that."

Stuttering now, the senator asked, "D-did you have something to do with Shavona's illness?"

Smirking at him, she said, "Did you think I was going to let you sleep with me without ever making a commitment. And you couldn't commit yourself to me as long as Shavona was still living and pressuring you to live some Godly life."

"How dare you. I could kill you," the senator growled as he lunged toward her.

Liza pulled the trigger and Senator Allen clutched his chest and then fell at her feet.

# Chapter 14

RaShawn had done nothing but pray after reaching out to Marcus and his dad. But as the taxi was nearing his destination, he realized that he should have done one more thing. He lifted his cell phone to call the police and saw that he had no battery life left. He then asked the cab driver if he could borrow his cell for a moment.

The cab driver looked at him skeptically but he relented.

RaShawn quickly dialed 911, gave them the address that Raven had given him and reported a disturbance in the house.

"What kind of disturbance?" the operator asked, in a calm, reassuring kind of voice.

"Someone is being held there against their will."

"And who would that be?"

RaShawn knew that the operator was just doing her job, but all these questions were annoying. The taxi pulled up to the house and he had no more time for twenty questions. "Just send someone in a hurry, please." He hung up and handed the phone back to the cabbie.

RaShawn paid the man and then jumped out of the car. His sister was inside and although he was thankful that the cops were on the way, he had no time to wait for them. He would just take his chances with Jesus.

***

"You shot him." Marcus dropped down next to his father. "Dad, are you okay... say something."

"I should have shot him a long time ago." Liza felt no sympathy for the man she married and planned to spend the rest of her life with. But her real venom was for his son and now that her husband was no longer in the way, she was about to unleash all the fury she had left in her.

"Why did you do it? Why couldn't you have just left our family alone?" Tears streamed down Marcus' face as he held on to the lifeless body of his hero. He knew that his father wasn't perfect, but that hadn't stopped him from loving and respecting the man.

"Watch out, Marcus," Raven yelled. From within her cage she could see black tentacle-like arms coming out of Liza's body and the finger nails being implanted into Marcus's scalp.

Marcus' hands went to his head. "It hurts, it hurts real bad, Raven. Pray for me."

"Her prayers will do you no good today," Liza barked, her voice sounding deeper than it normally did. "I told you before that you were our golden boy. Nothing has changed. I didn't spend all those years married to your father just to give up the vision that we have for you."

"I don't want any part of your vision," Marcus said as he closed his eyes trying to stop the exploding pain that was entering his brain.

"I am your vision, Marcus. Don't you understand anything yet? For almost twenty years I have given you and your father every vision you've come up with. Then you go and marry little miss holy ghost over there and think that you're going to stop me. Not possible, so let me tell you what you're going to do, if you want your little wife to remain alive."

"Don't hurt her. I'll do whatever you want." Marcus was trying his best to fight back against the pain, but he didn't have the strength.

"No," Raven yelled from within her cage. "You promised me, Marcus… you promised me."

He knew that she wanted him to be her *Phinehas,* he wanted that too. But it was so hard to keep that promise with a gun to his head and the threat of harm to his family. He wanted to stand up and do what was right. Rather the people of this world knew it or not, they needed someone to stand up for truth. But could he follow the cause of Christ at the risk of losing everything?

Raven started praying for him. "Oh Lord, give him strength to stand in this wicked and evil day. Lead him, Lord and guide him. Let him become everything you called him to be. In the name of Jesus," At that point, Britney and Rita joined in the prayer also.

Liza wasn't fazed, she held control over Marcus and knew it. She told him, "You're going to rehire Brian and you're going to get Christians to accept the Unity First agenda and then my lord, Satan will have finally won this battle, and your God will simply have to watch all the idiot humans he created be taken over by sin, including the vilest sin that anyone has ever imagined."

Marcus' mind drifted back to those days of his youth when he sat on his mother's lap and she spoke into his life. She'd called him a man of God. One that would fight to see God's will be done. He couldn't turn back, not even if he wanted to. Marcus turned toward Raven, wanting her lovely face to be the last thing he saw before death overtook him. With tears in his eyes, he proclaimed, "I won't do it. I was born to bring God's agenda back to this ungodly world. I won't go back on my promise."

"Then I'll kill you."

As Liza lifted the gun, RaShawn entered the basement. His hands were outstretched as he called on the name of Jesus. "Satan, you have no legal right to be here. All the forces of heaven are against you, so back to the pits of hell will you go. No demonic forces will have dominion over this man of God. You will not cause him to pervert this generation. But God has sent him to it to exalt His holy name."

The tentacles released Marcus and he dropped to the ground, still holding his head. Liza swung around to face off with RaShawn. She looked at him, trying to pinpoint the sin in his life so that the demonic forces within her could control him. But she could find no sin in this man. Fear clenched her heart as she backed away from him.

RaShawn advanced on her, his hands still outstretched. "In Jesus' name I command that you come out, you diabolical demon from the very pit. You have convinced this woman that there is pleasure in sin and that the world loves nothing more than to sin against God. But I have come to call you a liar. There are many in this world who desire to see the kingdom of God and to do His will. So, we banish you now and declare God's will in this situation. Thank you, Lord Jesus, for sending your angels to escort this demon back from whence he came."

Raven had never been more proud of her baby brother than the moment she actually witnessed two angels come as RaShawn had commanded. They pulled the demon out of Liza's body and then disappeared with him screaming and cackling all the way.

Liza slumped to the floor next to the senator. As she turned over her husband's lifeless body, all she could do was lay atop him and cry.

But she didn't have long to cry, because the police swarmed into the basement within the next few minutes, handcuffed Liza and unlocked the cages and set them all free. However, Raven sorta thought that Jesus had already set them free about an hour ago when each of them prayed like nothing else mattered.

*** 

The senator had been laid to rest, and Joe was still in critical condition, but Raven had high hopes that he would pull through. She had witnessed so many things in that basement that Raven didn't think she could be surprised by anything else in life. But when Judge Hartman stormed into her office screaming at her after she had brought her daughter home safe, Raven wondered if a demon was lurking somewhere within this woman who claimed to know God.

"I don't understand why you're upset; you told me you wanted your daughter back. My associate and I moved heaven and earth to get her for you. Joe is in critical condition right now because of how hard he worked on your behalf, and you're angry? I don't get it."

"I didn't expect her to be pregnant. I already had to deal with the shame of her being an addict, now it's all over the news that my daughter was held in a torture chamber of sorts because she had an affair and got pregnant by a senator."

"Those are the facts, Judge Hartman. Maybe you should try to talk with Britney to find out why she has been leading such a destructive life. Maybe then the two of you can find some peace."

Judge Hartman rolled her eyes heavenward. "I don't have time to talk to Britney. I have a campaign to salvage, no thanks to you." She left her office in a huff.

Raven sat there trying to figure out what had just happened when Marcus walked into her office. He was grinning. She enjoyed seeing that smile on his face, especially since he hadn't been smiling much lately.

"You can laugh at me if you want, but I don't understand what that woman is so mad about."

"I tried to tell you, but you wouldn't listen. Britney and I grew up together, so I know how she got so messed up. The wonderful Judge Hartman knew that her husband had been molesting Britney, but did nothing about it because he helped her to get her first seat on the bench. Then the woman got religion, but I don't think she's ever made peace with what she did to her daughter."

"That's sad, real sad." Raven put her hand over her belly and said, "Our baby is going to come first, before your political career and before my business. I won't allow anything to harm her."

"Or him," Marcus corrected.

"Whatever, I'm having a girl. I can feel it."

"If you say so. Are you ready to go?"

Raven bit down on her lip as she took a moment. Then said, "I just don't know if I should leave town right now with Joe still in critical condition."

"Joe is going to be all right. I have the best doctors in the field looking after him. You can't miss your brother's wedding."

"Oh yes I can. They want me to be a bridesmaid again, and I really don't feel like it. I know I shouldn't be such a brat because you are a wonderful man to be married to, but I didn't get my wedding, so I just don't feel like going to someone else's... not now."

"Your family will never get over it if you don't show up," Marcus told her.

"There are five of us, and extra husbands and wives to go around; they won't miss us."

Marcus put his hand to his head and sat down.

"What's wrong?" Raven jumped up. "You're not getting another headache, are you?" She started squinting, trying to see if any tentacles were going into his skull.

"No, but if you don't go to Raleigh with me, I think I'm going to end up with one. I purchased our tickets and took the time off from work. All I need you to do is agree. Your family really needs to see you."

"Okay, okay. If it's that important to you. I'll go, but you'll have to drive me home first because I haven't packed a thing."

"I already have your things packed. I shipped them to your parents' house a week ago."

"Why would you do that?"

"I didn't want to be bothered with luggage. This way we can just get on and off the plane as quickly as possible."

"All right, I'm coming, but if I have to be a bridesmaid again, then you owe me a wedding, buster... with all the trimmings."

"You got it," he told her with a sneaky grin on his face.

# Chapter 15

When she arrived at her parent's house everyone swarmed around, hugging her and telling her how terrified they were when they heard about what she was going through. Raven didn't want her family to worry about her, so she played it down, "It wasn't so bad. God was with me through it all. And I felt your prayers."

"One dead and another in critical condition," Renee said as she came over to the group. "I'd say it was something to worry about. But I'm so glad that God was there for you." Renee knew a little something about God showing up just when she needed Him most, because He'd been there for her when her ex-boyfriend stalked her and finally kidnapped and tormented her.

The sisters hugged, and then Nia brought a box into the family room for Raven to open. "Your husband mailed this here for you. So, you might want to open it."

Raven glanced at Marcus as she pulled the tape off the box. "I still don't understand why you mailed our clothes rather than letting me pack."

"Just open the box, and stop complaining," Marcus joked.

"I'm getting there." Raven pulled the final piece of tape off the box and then opened the flaps wide. With confusion etched across her face, Raven reached into the box and pulled out the most beautiful sparkling white wedding dress. She'd seen this dress before, but honestly, it looked much better in person than on the pages of a Vogue magazine.

As she turned towards him with questioning eyes, Marcus said, "I found your wedding book."

"But I don't understand. Why did you send my wedding dress here?"

Nia stepped forward just then and held out her ring finger. "I don't think I had a chance to show you this."

Raven glanced at her finger and noted that she was no longer just wearing her engagement ring, but the wedding band also. "Why do you have your band on, you and Ronny aren't getting married until tomorrow."

"No sis," Ronny said as he stepped forward and pulled Nia close to him. "Nia and I got married this morning in our pastor's office."

Raven shook her head, trying but failing miserably at understanding what was going on in this house. "Then why did Marcus and I come down here if you two are already married?"

Marcus stepped forward this time. He took Raven's hand in his and then bowed down on one knee. "I know I didn't handle things right when we got married. I rushed you and didn't allow you to have all the things you desired for your big day. Let me make that up to you now."

Tears streamed down Raven's face as Marcus added, "I love you so much, Raven. Would you please marry me again?"

"Did you say you love me?"

Marcus stood up, took Raven's face in his hand and pulled her close to him. He kissed her with all the hunger and desire he felt and then he said, "You heard right, Mrs. Allen. Your husband loves you more than anything and I just want to make you happy."

"In that case... let's get married."

***

Not only did Marcus have her dress delivered but he'd even ordered the bride's maid dresses for her sisters and had them mailed to their homes. "I can't believe this is happening," Raven said as she twirled around in her beautiful gown. Her sisters were dressed in the soft pink gowns that were almost exactly like the one she had picked out for them almost ten years ago.

Raven went over to Nia, who had agreed to be a bride's maid on the day that was supposed to be her wedding day. "I can't believe that you are doing this for me."

Nia waved the notion away. "I already had a big wedding, when I married my first husband. I don't need that anymore. All I want is a husband who is healthy and willing to live with me until we grow old and wrinkly together."

The two sister-in-laws hugged. "Thank you," Raven said again.

"Are you ready, honey," Ramsey asked as he stood at the door waiting to walk his daughter down the aisle. The moment was bitter-sweet because now that Raven was married, he'd run completely out of daughters to walk down the aisle.

"I'm ready daddy." She grabbed hold of his arm and went all in as she watched Maxine and Ramsey's daughter

Brielle sprinkle flower pedals on the floor and then one by one, Joy, Renee and then Nia marched down the aisle as her bride's maids just as she had done on countless occasions for them and others. But today was her day.

Exhaling, Raven slowly walked down the aisle. Mama-Carmella was smiling, Raven could imagine her saying, "I told you so. I knew that God had someone prepared for you."

And Raven would agree with her step-mother. Because her prince was waiting for her. She saw the tears flowing down his face as he watched her inch closer and closer to him and she knew without a doubt that this was really and truly, finally the love she had been waiting for.

***

A year later, Raven was holding their son in her arms as the count came in. He hadn't won by a landslide but there were still enough people in their state who wanted simple family values back to vote him in for another term. Not only that, but the unemployment was down and the people seemed content with their lives.

In his acceptance speech, Marcus stood next to Raven and his son saying, "I wish my father was here today. I'd love for him to know that good Godly principles won out over all the ungodly obstacles my opponent threw my way."

The crowd cheered him on as Marcus lifted his eyes towards heaven. His mother was up there and he hoped she was watching over him, seeing that he hadn't forgot the things she taught him. Her time on earth had been short, but necessary. "I thank God for the angel who birthed me and for the angel who gave birth to my son. And I promise you all that we will raise him with Godly values. The world talks a lot about separation of church and state. And I'm no preacher," he looked back at RaShawn who had been with him during the entire campaign, "I leave the preaching to my brother-in-law. But I am a man of faith, and if you'll allow me to guide this state in the manner I believe my faith dictates, I can guarantee you that will be able to clean up these streets from violence and drug abuse. Will be able to reunited wayward mothers with their children once again. If we bring back family values, my friends, this nation will once again rise and once again be the glory of the world."

Raven beamed with pride for her husband. He was a do-right kind of man. Someone she would be able to trust and so would the nation. He wouldn't do them harm just to score political points. Marcus Allen had her vote for whatever office he chose to run for. She would be with him, for every and always.

The End.

To My Readers,

This story was conceived after I read an article about a Christian organization that decided to go against the word of God and accept the things that man claims are right and true. But here is what the bible says about that:

*Brethren, be followers together of me, and mark them which walk so, as ye have us for an example. For many walk, of whom I have told you often, and now tell you even weeping, that they are the enemies of the cross of Christ: Whose end is destruction, whose God is their belly, and whose glory is in their shame, who mind earthly things. For our conversation is in heaven; from whence also we look for the Savior, the Lord Jesus Christ... Philippians 3: 17-20*

Naturally, after reading that article, my heart was heavy, but then I went to Sunday service and an elder at my church preached about Phinehas out of the 25th chapter of the book of Numbers. And suddenly I had my answer, if more of us would be like Phinehas and refuse to allow sin to have a place in the life of believers then we would be able to do some serious damage to the kingdom of darkness.

With the state the world is now in, I truly believe that the Lord is preparing to come back for His church... will you be ready? Or will you allow the god's of this world to penetrate your mind and move you so far away from the word of God that you'll no longer be able to tell the difference between right and wrong? I hope and pray that you will chose life rather than death, chose to be a Phinehas and stand up for God's truth and righteousness. I'm doing my part by writing this book. But you can do yours by praying for those who you can plainly see need a Savior. Don't hold the truth of God hostage inside of you. Share it with others.

I hope you enjoyed the eighth book in the Praise Him Anyhow series, I truly poured my heart and soul into it. We only have one novella left in this series... RaShawn the powerful warrior for God will have the final say. So, we will be ending this series on a high note of praise, as it should be.

Until we meet again, Your friend,

Vanessa

Sample Chapters of :

# *Song of Praise*

by

# Vanessa
# Miller

# Prologue

Looking out of the window from the twenty-first floor of his hotel room, RaShawn Thomas watched the people go about their business. Carrying packages, coming in and out of restaurants, smiling and laughing as they walked the streets. The people didn't seem the least bit aware of the destruction that was to come. But as sure as the flood waters of hurricane Katrina devastated New Orleans, and as sure as a tsunami could ravage and cripple a nation before they even knew what hit them, so too would be the way of the destruction that was to come. All that was required to turn back God's planned destruction was for the people to repent, but sadly, this nation and others like it was taking pleasure in their sins. They thought they had won, and that the truth of God had lost. Not realizing that God doesn't bow to any man or any sin, no matter how the world tries to dress it up.

Last night as he opened his Bible and turned to Jeremiah 51:20, RaShawn felt as if the Lord was speaking directly to him as he read:

*Thou art my battle axe and weapons of war: for with thee will I break in pieces the nations, and with thee will I destroy kingdoms.*

RaShawn had no understanding as to how he would break nations or destroy kingdoms, but he knew for sure that the Lord had ordered his steps all the way to Washington, DC. When his sister, Raven had called and asked him to come to Richmond, Virginia to be a spiritual advisor for her husband, Marcus Allen, he'd wondered then what God was up to. His brother-in-law had won the election and as governor of Virginia, Marcus and Raven were doing the Lord's work and doing right by the people in their state.

When RaShawn received the call concerning his new assignment, he felt as if God had released him from watching his brother-in-law's back. God had Marcus, and now the Lord was sending him on a new mission.

RaShawn had started his ministry service on the mission field. While doing the Lord's work in one country after the next, he had encountered demonic forces that tried to stop his mission. But God had always made a way of escape for RaShawn. As he left the hotel and walked down the street towards his new assignment, a chill went through RaShawn's body as he felt the presence of demonic forces that were much stronger than any he had ever encountered.

Looking up to heaven, RaShawn silently prayed, *Lord, be my strength.*

As he entered the church, RaShawn clearly heard the Lord respond.

**I will, now go forth and be my battle axe.**

The senior bishop of the fellowship met him in the entryway, shook his hand and said, "You made it safely, good. Come on in."

"Before we get started," RaShawn began as they walked down the hall towards his new office, "I'd just like to thank you for selecting me for this position."

Senior Bishop David Brown opened the door to the office and said, "I don't think you'll be thanking me once you see the mess you've inherited."

# Chapter One

*Be not conformed to this world: but be ye transformed by the renewing of your mind, that ye may prove what is that good and acceptable and perfect will of God.*
(Romans 12:2)

*Murder isn't so hard*, the killer thought, looked at the lifeless body of the victim the killer felt no remorse. How could one feel remorse when murder hadn't actually been committed—this was an assisted suicide. The man's sins had killed him. Now the Avenger of Sins, AKA the killer, sat down at the sinful man's desk and turned on the computer. The Avenger of Sins opened the man's email box and wrote a quick note, addressing it to Bishop RaShawn Thomas and put the killers real name on the signature line. The Avenger gasped as the name appeared on the computer screen, but then hit the backspace key several times.

Done with the email the Avenger clicked the Send button. The Avenger then walked back over to the dead man to spit on the body. But then thought about DNA, and what a shame it would be if the Avengers deeds were discovered because of something done on impulse. If that happened the Avenger wouldn't be able to finish the mission. And if the mission failed, then the Avenger wouldn't be able to exist—for after all, the Avenger was born to set the captives free. Instead of spitting on the dead man, the Avenger of Sins lifted a foot and kicked him in the ribs. The killer wanted to stomp him, but the Avenger remembered a show on Court TV where a killer was discovered because his shoe print was at the crime scene. The Avenger loved Reality TV; they always provided such good information.

The Avenger put the calling card on top of the body. Walking out of the room, the Avenger smiled as the thought of how much better the world would be with one more dead preacher.

***

"No. No, this is not happening. Not again," Bishop RaShawn Thomas said as he read his email. Some maniac was killing off the preachers within his fellowship and sending him emails about the awful deed. RaShawn had called the police immediately after receiving the last two emails, but it hadn't done him any good. By the time the police arrived at the homes of Pastor William Johnson and Pastor Nicolas Brown they were already dead. So RaShawn wasn't waiting this time. He would call the police on his way to Pastor Tony Hartman's home.

RaShawn grabbed his keys and then jumped into his Range Rover, all the while praying that he wasn't too late. Tony Hartman had given him more trouble than any of the preachers within his fellowship. The man was arrogant, self-serving and a womanizer; all of which served as the reasons RaShawn had asked the man to step down from his position. Since he'd taken over as bishop he'd asked a total of six pastors to step down.

RaShawn was a man with a true heart for God and therefore, he wanted to work with pastors who had the same hunger and passion that he had. The thought of a preacher misusing the children of God turned his stomach. He'd sat silently by and watched these so-called men of God work their way through ministries all his life. They destroyed lives and turned saints away from God with their lust for immorality and greedy ambitions. RaShawn had promised God that if he ever led a fellowship, he would get rid of every pimping preacher and womanizing minister that crossed his path. However, RaShawn never imagined that his goal of clearing out immorality amongst the leadership would result in murder.

Speeding down Interstate 285 headed to Tony's house, RaShawn pulled out his cell phone. He dialed Detective Jarod Harris' cell number. Detective Harris had been assigned to Pastor William Johnson's case and then subsequently assigned to Pastor Nicolas Brown's case. After Brown's murder, Detective Harris had handed RaShawn his business card and said, "If you run into any more dead preachers, call my cell phone."

RaShawn had hoped the detective's comment was nothing more than a bad joke and that he would never need to talk to Jarod Harris again in life, but here he was, waiting for the detective to answer the phone.

"Detective Harris."

RaShawn heard the greeting and almost hung up. He had never been through anything like this in all his life. He had grown up in ministry, and in all his thirty-two years, had never heard of a preacher being murdered in his own home.

"This is Detective Harris; is anyone there?"

"Oh, yes, Detective. This is Bishop RaShawn Thomas."

"Don't tell me that another one of your preachers has gotten himself killed."

Not wanting to accept that Pastor Tony was actually dead, RaShawn only confirmed, "I just received another email."

"Who is it this time?" Jarod asked, sounding a little irritated.

"The email was about Pastor Tony Hartman."

"Tony Hartman! I watch his program, *This is Your Moment* all the time," Jarod said, sounding a little more interested now.

"Can you meet me at his house?"

"Yeah. What's his address?"

RaShawn gave the detective the address and then hung up the phone. He was saddened by the shock in Detective Harris' tone, but a lot of people would be shocked to know that the same preacher who taught millions how to claim their moment and how to always be in the midst of God's perfect timing was the same man who regularly solicited prostitutes and had been carrying on a three-year affair with a stripper named Peaches.

RaShawn prayed that Tony was still alive as he pulled up behind the man's Bentley, jumped out of his SUV and began pounding on the front door. "Tony, are you in there?"

He knocked on the door several more times, calling Tony's name without receiving a response. Tony's wife, Carla had divorced him a year ago, so RaShawn didn't expect that she would open the door or be in the house to help Tony in his time of need. He grabbed the door knob and turned it. The door opened. But instead of RaShawn rejoicing, he inwardly cringed because he knew that Tony never left his door unlocked. Checking each room one by one, RaShawn kept calling Tony's name.

When he reached Tony's home office towards the back of the house on the first floor, RaShawn found Tony stretched out on the floor. He ran to the preacher and knelt down beside him. He lifted his wrist to feel for a pulse. RaShawn then noticed two things at once: There was no pulse and there was a note card lying on Tony's chest. The card had a message. It read, *You do right, and I won't do wrong.*

"Bishop Thomas, are you in here?"

RaShawn heard Detective Harris as he entered the house. He wanted to go greet the man but he didn't want to leave Tony. That fact was ironic to him now, since a couple of weeks ago he wanted to not just get far away from Tony, but to strip the man of his license to preach the gospel. "I'm in here," he hollered.

"Is he dead?" Detective Harris asked as he entered the room.

RaShawn nodded.

"Does he have a card on his chest?"

RaShawn nodded again.

"Did you touch it?"

"No. It was right side up on his chest. I was able to read what it says without touching it." RaShawn turned to Detective Harris with a stunned expression on his face. "Was this note on the other bodies as well?"

"Yes, but we haven't released that information to the public." Detective Harris stepped toward the body as he said, "You shouldn't be in here."

"I had hoped to find him alive." RaShawn rubbed his forehead with the palm of his hand as he stood up. "I honestly don't know how much more of this I can take. I don't understand why this maniac has decided to kill the pastors I fired."

"You fired Pastor Hartman! The man was an icon. I didn't think anyone but God had the authority to fire a man like him."

RaShawn lowered his head as his shoulders slumped.

Putting a hand on the bishop's shoulder, Jarod said, "You can't blame yourself, Bishop. Whoever killed these men did exactly what he wanted to do."

There was no blood. But RaShawn hadn't expected to see any. Detective Harris hadn't communicated much about the other two men's deaths, but he had informed RaShawn that the preachers had been poisoned. RaShawn looked around the room, trying to discover what someone could have used to poison Tony. His eyes drifted to a bottle of grape juice, crumpled crackers and a single wine glass on the desk in Tony's home office. "The poison is in the grape juice, isn't it?"

"In the last two cases the poison had only been in the glass, but not in the bottle of grape juice," Detective Harris said, and then quickly added, "That does not leave this room. We haven't released that information to the public either."

RaShawn turned back toward Tony Hartman and rubbed his forehead with his palm again.

"I'm going to call this in," Detective Harris said. "I need you to wait in the living room so I can question you once I get things in order. And try not to beat me to the next crime scene. Okay?"

Bishop RaShawn wearily walked out of the room and sat down in the living room as he was instructed. He didn't plan to beat Detective Harris to the next crime scene, because RaShawn hoped and prayed that there wouldn't be another one. He had every intention of begging and pleading for police protection for the last three preachers that he recently fired.

He waited while Detective Harris ushered other police officers and forensic technicians into the crime scene. He was sure that Detective Harris would want to speak with him once they had taken care of Tony, so he just kept waiting. RaShawn wished he had remembered to bring the email that he'd received, but the last two emails hadn't provided much of anything to go on. The person sending the messages used a different computer and location with each message.

RaShawn watched as one of the detectives carried the grape juice and wine glass out in a Ziplock bag. It was somehow out of place to see just one wine glass with grape juice. After all, it wasn't actual wine that Tony had been drinking, which he was sure the man indulged in privately. But why would he drink grape juice in a wine glass by himself? RaShawn associated grape juice with communion. Would Tony have taken communion by himself or did the killer also drink it? That would explain why the bottle wasn't tainted. The killer must have poured the poison in Tony's glass and then had communion with him. *But why communion?* RaShawn wondered.

The Bible clearly states in I Corinthians 11:27, "Whosoever shall eat this bread, and drink this cup of the Lord, unworthily, shall be guilty of the body and blood of the Lord." Is that what the mad man was trying to tell them?

RaShawn had no problem understanding the note that was left on Tony's body, but this communion thing was a mystery to him. A murderer and a whore-monger had no reason to partake in communion, did they?

"There's a camera crew outside. You might want to give his next of kin a quick call before they hear about this on the news," Detective Harris told RaShawn as he walked into the living room.

"Me? But I fired the man. His sister was smoking mad at me for that; no way does she want to hear from me right now."

"I can do it myself, but it's going to be a while. I just thought you might want to beat the afternoon news." Detective Harris nodded toward the big picture window in the living room.

RaShawn looked outside and saw just what the detective had been referring to. Camera crews from several news stations were lining the street just below

Tony's driveway. He turned back around and said, "I'll call her."

RaShawn took out his cell phone, dreading the call he had to make to Judge Lisa Hartman. But as he began punching in the number, RaShawn changed his mind about which Hartman he would call. Tony's niece, Britney and RaShawn had history. Two years ago, he and his sister, Raven had saved Britney from a crazy lady who'd wanted to kill her because she'd made the mistake of not only sleeping with the woman's husband, but getting pregnant by him. The ordeal had caused Britney to miscarry.

After the miscarriage, Britney decided to no longer wallow in the pain of her past and got busy cleaning up her act. She was now working as an insurance fraud investigator. She and her mother still weren't on the best of terms, due to her past behavior, but maybe something like this could help to bring mother and daughter back together.

Even knowing that he should call Judge Hartman, it mattered more to RaShawn to find out how this whole thing would affect Britney. He dialed her number and waited for her to pick up. When she did, there was laughter in her voice and RaShawn hated that he was about to take the joy she had found away from her.

You've been reading an excerpt of:
Song of Praise (Book 9)

# About the Author

Vanessa Miller is a best-selling author, playwright, and motivational speaker. She started writing as a child, spending countless hours either reading or writing poetry, short stories, stage plays and novels. Vanessa's creative endeavors took on new meaning in 1994 when she became a Christian. Since then, her writing has been centered on themes of redemption, often focusing on characters facing multi-dimensional struggles.

Vanessa's novels have received rave reviews, with several appearing on *Essence Magazine's* Bestseller's List. Miller's work has receiving numerous awards, including "Best Christian Fiction Mahogany Award" and the "Red Rose Award for Excellence in Christian Fiction." Miller graduated from Capital University with a degree in Organizational Communication. She is an ordained minister in her church, explaining, "God has called me to minister to readers and to help them rediscover their place with the Lord."

Vanessa has recently completed the For Your Love series for Kimani Romance and How Sweet the Sound for Abingdon Press, first book in a historical set in the Gospel era which releases March 2014. Vanessa is currently working on an ebook series of novellas in the Praise Him Anyhow series. She is also working on the My Soul to Keep series for Whitaker House.

Vanessa Miller's website address is: **www.vanessamiller.com** But you can also stay in touch with Vanessa by joining her mailing list @ **http://vanessamiller.com/events/join-mailing-list/** Vanessa can also be reached at these other sites as well:

Join me on Facebook: https://www.facebook.com/groups/77899021863/

Join me on Twitter: https://www.twitter.com/vanessamiller01

98347850R00085

Made in the USA
Columbia, SC
23 June 2018